"Why?"

Garrett crossed his arms. "Why did you only want one date?"

Olivia shut her eyes. This was so horrible. She'd ruined everything. How could she ever have thought a one-night stand was a good idea? Bad girls had bad ideas.

"The truth," he demanded.

Her eyes flew open. "I…"

"Did you plan to seduce me?" The question hit like a harsh accusation.

"It seemed the answer to my problem."

"You mean the virginal Olivia Jacobsen problem?"

It was out there now, what she'd done, and it rang tawdry and crass. Which was exactly how Garrett took it. What could she say? How could she make this better?

The silence stretched. Finally he spoke, each word like a knife.

"Tell me, Olivia. Be honest just this once. How much of you is real—and how much is a lie?"

Dear Reader,

I am delighted to finally bring you Olivia Jacobsen's story and finish the Jacobsen family saga that I started what seems aeons ago. For Olivia, being a "bad girl" is about as far out of character as this minister's daughter can get. However, she's not going to turn thirty-one without a fight, and she plans to liven up her boring life and have some fun, if only for one night. When sexy cop Garrett Krause kisses her breath away, however, she discovers that one night isn't enough, and she wonders if she can turn one night into forever. But there's this little matter of some lies she's told that could ruin everything.

If you've ever dreamed of being someone else or pretended to be, if only for a moment, you'll empathize with Olivia Jacobsen as she struggles to find true love. With some well-meaning meddling from Grandpa Joe, I can promise you the family saga comes to an exciting and satisfying conclusion.

It's hard to say goodbye to these characters, and I hope you enjoy their story as much as I did creating it. The road to love is often paved with good intentions, but sometimes, as Olivia will find out, you simply need a little faith.

As always, enjoy the romance, and feel free to e-mail me at michele@micheledunaway.com with any feedback.

Michele Dunaway

P.S. Jacobsen characters are also found in *Catching the Corporate Playboy* (Darci), *The Playboy's Protegee* (Harry), and *About Last Night...* (Shane).

CAPTURING
THE COP
Michele Dunaway

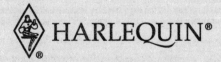

HARLEQUIN®

TORONTO • NEW YORK • LONDON
AMSTERDAM • PARIS • SYDNEY • HAMBURG
STOCKHOLM • ATHENS • TOKYO • MILAN • MADRID
PRAGUE • WARSAW • BUDAPEST • AUCKLAND

ISBN 0-373-75120-6

CAPTURING THE COP

www.eHarlequin.com

Printed in U.S.A.

To Cornbread, WIL92, whose voice wakes me up
each morning—kudos for all you do for our
troops and for my hometown of St. Louis.
To Dale Earnhardt, Jr., you've given me a reason
to discover NASCAR and become a fan. Thanks also
to the Warren Brothers for proving that it's okay to
be barely famous. You've provided fantastic music to
write by. Thanks to all of you for being inspirations.

Acknowledgment

Special acknowledgment goes to
Officer Ed Ucinski, my personal friend, and to
O'Fallon Police Department Detective Jimmy Klinger,
who graciously answered all my questions
regarding the Major Case Squad, of which he is a
member. For information on The BackStoppers,
please visit www.backstoppers.org.

Books by Michele Dunaway

HARLEQUIN AMERICAN ROMANCE

848—A LITTLE OFFICE ROMANCE
900—TAMING THE TABLOID HEIRESS
921—THE SIMPLY SCANDALOUS PRINCESS
931—CATCHING THE CORPORATE PLAYBOY
963—SWEEPING THE BRIDE AWAY
988—THE PLAYBOY'S PROTÉGÉE
1008—ABOUT LAST NIGHT...
1044—UNWRAPPING MR. WRIGHT
1056—EMERGENCY ENGAGEMENT
1100—LEGALLY TENDER

Chapter One

Inside every good girl is a bad girl waiting to get out. Unfortunately for Olivia Jacobsen, she'd been waiting thirty years.

She studied herself in the mirror of the twenty-fifth-floor executive washroom. There was nothing "bad" about her appearance, in as far as she could tell. She had blue eyes. She had straight dark hair, a gift from her deceased Greek mother. Today Olivia had pushed her shoulder-length hair back with a pink plaid headband that matched her pleated plaid skirt.

The saleslady at the upscale boutique had insisted that head-to-toe plaid was the latest fashion, but now Olivia wasn't so sure.

She scowled at her reflection. Fashion be darned. She came across like a pupil at one of St. Louis's all-girl Catholic high schools. Olivia Jacobsen—thirty-year-old Miss Goody Two-shoes.

Worse, she was a thirty-year-old *virgin* Goody Two-shoes, the perfectly behaved daughter of Blake and

Sara Jacobsen, world-famous evangelicals with an international ministry rivaling that of Billy Graham.

And she'd grown up hearing exactly what being bad got you.

Olivia puckered her lips, making another disgusted face at herself in the mirror. Being good was boring. Being good meant broken engagements because she'd gotten cold feet—well, that and the fact that kissing her two respective fiancés had been like kissing puppies. Cute and sloppy, but hardly satisfying. Being good also meant having a stepmother who watched your every move and a meddling family that constantly tried to marry you off to someone they deemed appropriate—someone bland and boring.

Being good meant never having a man touch your breasts, never once feeling the leg-clenching desire that Olivia read about in those romance novels her minister parents disapproved of but she devoured.

Just once, Olivia Jacobsen wanted to be bad. She wanted to sin. She shook her body to try to loosen it up. It was a pathetic attempt, and at that moment Olivia decided she couldn't continue like this. Something drastic would have to be done.

No longer would she be lackluster Olivia Jacobsen, staid and sedate long before her time. That ended now. She reached for her plaid purse and strolled purposefully out of the washroom.

"Marilyn?"

Upon hearing Olivia's voice, her secretary glanced up.

"I'm going to take the rest of the day off," Olivia said. "Please reschedule all my appointments."

If Marilyn seemed surprised that Olivia Jacobsen, vice president of corporate communications for Jacobsen Enterprises and the one with the flawless attendance record for the past five years, was ditching work early, she didn't let on. "Yes, Ms. Jacobsen," she replied with a neutral expression.

"I'll see you tomorrow." Not even bothering to return to her office, Olivia punched the elevator button and headed down.

Once-bitten, twice-shy DWM, blond-blue 6'3" HWP, 36 seeking a 26-34 HWP S/DWF for Ms. Right. Must understand erratic work shifts, must love kids, quiet family life and cats.

"I THINK YOU SHOULD mention that you're Mr. August. Or at least a cop. What about 'hot stuff'? Doesn't that increase your odds?"

Garrett Krause glared up from the almost illegible handwriting he'd scrawled on a torn-out sheet of white notebook paper. Not only was his partner, Cliff, reading over his shoulder, but he was also laughing at him.

"And I think you should butt out before I snuff you out," Garrett snapped, not at all surprised to hear himself growling like an angry bear. "It's your fault I'm in this mess in the first place. As if I want to do this."

Cliff simply laughed harder—a liberty only a good

friend could take, especially when the laughter was clearly at his friend's expense.

"You won't snuff me out," Cliff said. "We've been together too long. Besides, I know all the homicide detectives."

That was true, Garrett thought wryly. He and Cliff were both detectives in the Division of Criminal Investigation, specifically the Bureau of Crimes Against Persons. Although Cliff was older, he and Garrett had been best friends since they'd met in Police Academy. After that, they'd been stationed together and they'd even both made detective within months of each other. Later, both had landed positions as investigators on St. Louis's Major Case Squad.

Garrett often wondered if some of his career advancement had been due to Cliff—after all, Cliff's family was rich, and powerful in St. Louis politics. But Garrett didn't really care. He loved his job. He'd been a cop since graduating college, and cops shouldn't be writing personal ads.

"Lucky for you and your occupation that you get to live another day," Garrett snorted, not quite ready to let Cliff off so easily.

"Oh, I'm so worried," Cliff taunted. Cliff knew he could push Garrett's buttons—they had an eleven-year friendship, one that had included Cliff being best man for Garrett's now-failed marriage.

"I'm sure I could commit the perfect crime if I wanted to," Garrett threatened as he waved the paper. "Don't tempt me."

"Yeah, whatever. Besides, I'm always lucky," Cliff said, cuffing his white shirtsleeves. He ignored Garrett's scowl and reached for his mug. "I'd probably end up killing you in self-defense."

"Don't you have somewhere to be? An appointment?" Garrett asked, eyeing Cliff's Cops Do It shootin' expression mug. At least Cliff's sip of java had ended his annoying laughter.

"Aw, come on, Garrett, lighten up," Cliff said before taking another sip. "None of us means you any harm. We just agree that you should get back into dating. It's been three years since that ugly mess with your ex."

"Don't even mention her." Garrett's scowl deepened. Although three years had passed since his divorce, he still hated dealing with his ex-wife, especially where their four-year-old son was concerned.

Cliff tilted his head to the side and studied his friend. "Garrett, really. What's wrong with you? Everyone's more than a little concerned about your hermit status."

"I am not a hermit. I'm busy," Garrett insisted.

Cliff shook his head. "No, you aren't. You work hard, granted, but that's not what's bugging you."

Cliff contemplated that assertion for a moment and then his expression changed. "I got it. You're still smarting over that charity calendar. Come on, let it go. It's been almost a year since it debuted, and all the hubbub has died down. In a few months people will throw the thing away and replace it with next year's version."

"Whatever," Garrett said. As with his ex, he tried to avoid dwelling on that mistake, as well.

"Though I still think you're crazy," Cliff continued. "If I'd gotten one of those prime spots, can you imagine what I would have done?"

That was the last straw. "What—you'd have dated the woman from Potosi who sent me her underwear?" Garrett arched his eyebrow skeptically and studied his friend. It was now almost two p.m., and already Cliff needed to shave. Because Garrett was blond, his face wouldn't show a beard until well after five.

Cliff shrugged, conceding slightly. "Well, maybe not that," he said, retreating before going back for round two. "But some of those babes who dropped by the police station were hot. I would have taken the normal ones up on their offers. Wasn't one a Rams cheerleader? Get real, Garrett. Just hop back in the saddle again. Being celibate this long just doesn't suit a man. Makes him crack. God knows we see the results of that enough in our line of work."

Garrett glared. His self-chosen celibacy had so far suited him just fine. Being celibate meant he'd make no more mistakes such as thinking he was in love and the time was perfect for him to settle down. That was how he'd come to marry Brenda. The only good thing to emerge from that tempestuous relationship had been their son. And that adorable four-year-old deserved his daddy's full attention.

"Don't knock celibacy. It's the best alternative to marriage, that's for sure," Garrett said.

"Who said anything about marriage? Saddles are for riding in, buddy boy." Cliff grinned, but his smile vanished when he saw the sour expression on Garrett's face. "Oh, loosen up. At least none of us is trying to drag you out to strip clubs anymore under the guise of doing a stakeout."

Thank God for small favors, Garrett thought. Exploring East Saint Louis's "nightlife" was not anywhere on his to-do list, nor would it ever be. The Illinois city directly over the Mississippi River from the Gateway Arch was known for strip clubs and seedy bars—something he'd outgrown long ago. And since Garrett wasn't a gambler, even Casino Queen riverboat, decent as that was, held little appeal. He shook his head, sending blond hair into his face. Loosen up indeed. As if he could.

He shuddered, revulsion shivering down his spine as he remembered some of the women's letters and photos he'd received in the months following the appearance of the Hometown Heroes charity calendar.

Reading the letters and seeing the lengths women would go to to entice him, including those naked full-body shots, had not been pleasant. He'd felt like a pervert, so much so that he'd finally stopped opening the letters at all, or letting his cop buddies and Cliff raid his mail. Crime scenes were easier to deal with.

He winced. Hindsight was twenty/twenty. When the department asked for his cooperation last summer, Garrett had followed orders, not caring about the "honor" attached to being selected.

His mistake was that he hadn't thought through the calendar's aftereffects. Oh, he'd considered that he might get some recognition and second glances, but this was St. Louis and not Hollywood. St. Louisans were, for the most part, discreet—not rude autograph-seekers. Even professional sports stars were usually granted their privacy in public places like restaurants or movie theaters. The crazy attention paid to him and his fellow police, fire and rescue workers from across the metropolitan region had surprised Garrett, not to mention vexed him.

Today, it appeared, there would be no end to his weary annoyance. Cliff was on a mission he'd started this past weekend when Garrett lost the weekly Friday night poker game with the guys.

"Let me see that personal ad again," Cliff said, getting back to the matter at hand. He snagged the paper from Garrett. "HWP. That's good. You don't want someone whose height and weight aren't proportional. But, do you think it's a good idea to tell them your measurements?"

"Earlier you wanted me to tell them I was Mr. August so that they could go ogle me. Why don't I just include my address in the ad? Even better, how about I include my cell phone number and the note 'Call Garrett for a good time.'" Irritated, Garrett wrestled the piece of paper away from Cliff. "This is a dumb idea. I'm not doing it."

Cliff snatched the paper, ripping off a piece in the process. "Yes, you are. You backed yourself into a corner Friday night when Ben asked how long it had been since you'd had a real date. You even went double or nothing without chips—and lost. So unless you really want to eat crow—"

"I thought I had a good hand," Garrett interrupted. Two of a kind should have been enough to win.

"Well, you didn't, so even fate agrees you're doing this. You'll never live down the ribbing if you don't. It's a personal ad or a blind date."

The last blind date Garrett had gone on had been an absolute disaster. She'd been five years older and around the block way too many times, and had boldly asked him if he knew any kinky ways to use his handcuffs. No more blind dates, period.

"Fine, I said I'd do this," Garrett said with another growl to indicate that he still didn't relish the idea. "*One* date with *one* woman. That was the bet, and that's all I'm doing. Understood?"

Cliff's smile widened and he gave Garrett the crumpled piece of paper. "Okay. One date. That's the deal. But place the ad today. You'll pass by the *Monitor* office on your way home."

Garrett narrowed his eyes and glared. The *Monitor* office was actually out of his way, but Cliff, again intent on revising the ad's wording, disregarded his friend's displeasure.

"Don't forget to add 'no smoking,'" Cliff said. "Just in case you want to kiss her."

"I won't be kissing anyone," Garrett snapped, but he did write down n/s on the paper.

Cliff's laughter again echoed in the room. "No kisses? You never know, Garrett. You never know."

"OLIVIA! OH, AM I GLAD to see you!" Chrissy Lambert said as Olivia entered the classified-ads department of the *Mound City Monitor* on Tucker Street. Located on the first floor, the office was open to walk-in clients until six o'clock. Chrissy buzzed Olivia through the security door.

"Hi, Chrissy. I wanted to check on you personally." Olivia gave her best friend a quick hug.

"They were Braxton-Hicks contractions," Chrissy said as she hopped on one foot, clearly needing to go to the restroom. "You're a godsend. Lula called in sick today, which means she's more likely at the stadium playing hooky, than on her deathbed. I'm here alone."

Chrissy wiggled her very pregnant body. She was due any day now.

"Are you okay?" Olivia asked. She'd known Chrissy ever since junior high, when, despite their different socioeconomic backgrounds, they'd become best friends at Bible camp. Olivia's family had viewed the month-long adventure as a natural extension of their daughter's religious education; Chrissy's family had hoped that discovering God would tame their daughter's wild ways. The ultimate bad girl, Chrissy hadn't truly reformed until she met Derek, fallen fast for him and gotten married.

Chrissy palmed her stomach. "I'm doing well except for the baby having stationed itself right on top of my bladder. Watch the floor for me, will you? Don't worry, the bosses aren't around. Since the Cardinals lead the Central division, everyone cut out early to attend today's baseball game."

"No problem," Olivia said. "Besides, I know the paper's owner." Olivia's cousin Darci was married to Cameron O'Brien. In fact, Darci and Cameron had first met when Cameron, the head of O'Brien Publications, had visited St. Louis to finalize the purchase of the *Mound City Monitor* and add it to the O'Brien Publications family.

"That's great, 'cause I really gotta go. You know what to do, right?"

"You showed me last time," Olivia said. "Remember? It was so slow here we filled out phone ad forms pretending to find me a date."

"Yeah. Mr. B. Right at 4 M. Drives."

A movement outside on the sidewalk caught Chrissy's attention, and she paused for a moment. "Whoa! I don't believe it. That's really him. Too bad nature's calling. But you're about to get lucky. See that guy out there?"

Olivia glanced out the *Monitor*'s large storefront window. She saw the subject of Chrissy's focus immediately.

The man standing just outside the glass doorway was gorgeous. Under the dark blue T-shirt he wore, well-toned muscles rippled and the golden hair dusting his arms glistened in that late-afternoon sunlight. He stood at least six foot three, and even his faded red Cardinals baseball cap added to his allure.

Olivia swallowed. What would it be like to touch a man like that? Unlike Chrissy, who had more skeletons in her closet than were in a graveyard, Olivia had never been bad enough to know. Her wimpy ex-fiancés had been physically small men whose presence wouldn't intimidate a flea.

She fisted her hands, then stretched her fingers one by one in order to relax. The man seemed familiar, but Olivia couldn't place him. "Chrissy," she hissed as the man began to pull open the door to the office. "What are you talking about? You know him?"

"The calendar in the file drawer. He's one of the 'months.' Oh, too bad it's against the rules to get his autograph or hang it up." Chrissy paused for one last peek before hurrying away.

Whoever the man was, he was now inside the office, and Olivia couldn't help but gape as he approached the service counter.

Never had a man so filled the room with his presence. His dark blue Levi's fit tightly and he wore boots. Olivia stood rooted to the floor as he approached, her only movements those of her fingers as they twisted the strand of cultured pearls her father had given her for her twenty-fifth birthday. Brad Pitt, Dennis Quaid and Robert Redford combined wouldn't hold a candle to the Adonis before her. He must have come to place an ad, Olivia decided as she regrouped. Maybe he was selling his truck or something—although the *Mound City Monitor* really didn't handle many of those kind of classified ads.

Yes, Olivia fantasized, he would be the type to own a big truck.

He was wearing Levi's and boots and Olivia could picture him riding on the range, roping some cattle, coming home to his woman and making love to her on soft flannel sheets in front of the fire. He was the stuff of romance novels, the ultimate lover—which meant not her type. Besides, how could she handle a man like him? She wasn't even bad enough to find something bad to do. After leaving work and playing hooky, the only "bad" thing she could think of to do was shopping. Her one last ditch attempt at badness before heading home to a freezer full of microwavable dinners and bad television shows had been to visit Chrissy. All in all, not a great start at becoming a bad girl.

"I need to place a personal ad."

His warm baritone voice jerked Olivia into the present and her gaze connected with his. Since only a forty-inch counter and some Plexiglas stood between them, she could see that his eyes were a mesmerizing shade of blue.

Olivia had never understood what people meant when they said "time stood still," but at this moment she swore it was happening. Her heart seemed frozen, although she could feel it beating and could hear it pounding in her ears.

"A personal ad," he repeated, obviously irritated at her incompetence.

He drummed his fingers on the counter, the staccato sound forcing Olivia to regain her senses.

"Yes, of course. I'd be happy to help," she somehow managed to say. She couldn't have anyone complaining to the bosses about Chrissy.

"This is the ad I wish to run." He slid a wadded piece of paper into the metal channel and underneath the Plexiglas. "Can you take care of it?"

If she were a bad girl, she'd take care of him in any way he needed. *Be a bad girl*, something unfamiliar inside her whispered.

She smoothed out the paper and turned her attention to reading his ad. She glanced up sharply. "You need a date?"

His blue eyes gleamed, and she swallowed. Just the power of his look held her attention. "I apologize. That was quite unprofessional of me."

He didn't agree or disagree; he just watched her. Years of PR training came in handy as she hid her trembling and presented a poised appearance. She reached for an advertising form and a pen.

"So. How long do you want your ad to run? Our best value, which I suggest, is five days at five dollars a day. If not you can—"

He cut her off. "That's fine."

Olivia's forehead wrinkled and her headband itched. Something wasn't right in Mound City. Her extensive PR experience had also taught her a lot about body language.

For someone placing a personal ad, the man standing in front of her wasn't keen on the idea.

He came across like a man sitting in a dentist's chair, waiting for a tooth extraction. But whatever his problem, she had an ad to sell. "We have three re-trieval services, depending on what type of response you'd like," she said, warming to her sales pitch. She and Chrissy had held a contest to see who could say it faster. "You can place a voice-mail ad, meaning the person calls a special phone number and presses your mailbox number. You receive a code to retrieve the messages. For an additional fee, we can set up a tem-porary e-mail account for you, meaning we act as your firewall. You can also go with the traditional snail-mail option, which—"

"Which one gets this over with the fastest?"

His blunt query had Olivia losing her train of thought and flubbing her sales spiel. "The phone mes-sages," she said as she recovered. "The people inter-ested in you dial a nine-hundred number—you retrieve the messages using an eight-hundred number."

"Fine," he said with a curt nod that caused a lock of blond hair to fall into his face. "That's what I want for the shortest period you offer."

"One week."

He didn't smile. "Perfect."

She pushed the contract under the glass. "I'll need your contact information. If you could please fill this out…"

As he put pen to paper, Olivia couldn't help but watch him, observing the way his muscles flexed even when he did something so simple as write. He'd barely finished printing his first name in the required block letters when he glanced up at her.

"Is something wrong?"

"Yes," Olivia said, the words escaping her lips before she could even think to stop them. "Why does a gorgeous man like you need to place an ad?"

His blond eyebrows arched. "For the same reason a grown-up woman like you dresses like a Catholic schoolgirl."

"Fashion," Olivia retorted.

His unexpectedly wide smile undid her. It crooked into two dimples, lighting up his whole face. She gripped the countertop.

"No, the obvious," he said. "Because like everyone else who places these personal ads, I need a date. Just one, but a date nevertheless."

As his gaze remained locked with Olivia's, she inwardly melted. All those romance clichés fit. An invisible string tugged her insides and her toes curled. Blood drummed in her ears. The man had turned her into molten jelly with a mere glance. Made her feel wanton with only his simple, sexy manner.

At that moment, Olivia's inner bad girl roared to life and took over. She wanted to experience life to the fullest, right? This man would make her feel full, that was for certain. Many women had no doubt propositioned this beautiful, sexy man, but the prodigal daughter didn't care. He only needed one date.

She only needed one night.

She could atone for her many sins later.

Olivia turned on her best smile. Her baby blue-eyes with the outer rim of dark blue—the blue eyes that every Jacobsen family member shared—were her strongest feature, and she refused to blink. The husky voice leaving her lips sounded unfamiliar.

"So if you only need one date," Olivia said, "why not save your money and just ask me?"

Chapter Two

Had he heard her correctly? Had she just propositioned him? Garrett surveyed the woman behind the
counter. She'd finally blinked and glanced away, but
Garrett knew his excellent hearing hadn't failed him.
The girl who was doing her best to imitate the cover
of Britney Spears's first album had just made a pass
at him.

Was there a woman in the world who wouldn't?

He continued to study her as she placed some pens
in a holder. Admittedly, she seemed different from the
others who had hit on him. Very classic. Very traditional. She wore a short-sleeved pink sweater and had
pearls around her neck. Her dark hair fell to her shoulders. Her headband matched the pleated skirt he could
see because of his height. She had high cheekbones,
a straight nose that tweaked up slightly at the tip, and
her eyes…those blue orbs were hypnotic. He'd noticed
them the moment he'd walked into the office.

An urge stirred in his groin. Did he really want to

reach through the glass and feel how silky those dark locks were?

She definitely wasn't unattractive. Far from it.

But she had boldly propositioned him, and after this past year, Garrett was sick and tired of aggressive women. He couldn't wait until December, when, he hoped, everyone would throw this year's charity calendar away and instead ogle the people in the new one.

He couldn't go back to the station without arranging for a date. One date, to be precise. And if he took her up on her offer, he could have that one date without having to place a silly ad, or ever having some silly ad traced back to him.

He also wouldn't have to listen to any phone messages. He wouldn't have to call anyone up and make idle conversation he didn't have time for. Yes, the longer he considered asking out the counter girl, the more the idea appealed. Even better—since she was a counter girl, she certainly wouldn't have the upper-crust St. Louis snobbery of his ex-wife.

Having had women throw themselves at him, he'd long ago learned to turn his sexuality down. Now he let every ounce of his male magnetism loose. He leaned on the counter, bringing himself down to her five-eight height and as close to the Plexiglas as he could without causing condensation to form. "You mean you're offering to go out with me and be my one date? You don't even know what it's for."

He was glad to see that she blushed, a delightful

pink that spread across her face and almost matched her sweater. Miss Proposition wasn't as sure of herself as she had seemed. His cop's instinct noticed the incongruity and found it intriguing.

"I—" she began.

He didn't give her the chance to back down. "Do you fit my criteria?" He reached under the divider and withdrew the crumpled scrap of notebook paper. "Let's see, shall we? You appear to be between twenty-six and thirty-four."

"I'm thirty," the girl said.

She fidgeted with her fingers, and he noticed that she'd recently had a manicure.

"Thirty, huh?" He would have guessed she was much younger. Maybe because she didn't have on much makeup and wore that infernal headband. Then again, unlike his ex-wife, adornments for her weren't essential; she had a natural beauty, something internal, which he now knew Brenda had always lacked. He shifted his weight.

"Single or divorced?"

She coughed as she said, "Single."

"Look at me." She complied, and this time he decided her eyes were the most interesting shade of baby blue, even lighter than his. He tamped down immediate desire. Sure, he'd been celibate since his divorce, but his mission wasn't about desiring the counter girl. He had a quest to complete. The sooner he got the guys off his back, the sooner his life would return to normal.

"So, how are you with erratic work shifts, kids, quiet family life and cats?"

Her chin lifted defiantly. "I work full-time, my sister has two kids and my brother's baby is six months old. My family life is quiet and I had a seal-point Siamese when I was growing up."

"Then you'll be perfect." Even he heard the hoarse undertone in his voice.

"Yes."

Her chin trembled briefly, and the movement fascinated Garrett. Unlike the other women who'd propositioned him, she acted almost regretful. She was also cute and quaint, yet still downright sexy. Definitely kissable.

The paradox interested him. With her sweater and pearls she was a walking advertisement for prim and proper.

Somehow he couldn't picture the woman in front of him even exposing her navel in public the way some women did. Yet despite her classic clothes and reserved demeanor, she was doing something to his libido.

The way her lips parted like that. Without even recognizing she was making the movement, her tongue flicked out and wet her bottom lip. Garrett groaned inwardly. At this moment, he wanted nothing more than to break down the glass barrier between them and plant his lips on hers.

Maybe Cliff was correct. Maybe Garrett should get back in the saddle.

He pushed the *Mound City Monitor* classified ad form back toward her, the gesture providing his body some much-needed respite. "Since I need a date and you've offered, I guess I won't be using this." She blinked, and this time her long dark brown eyelashes held him captive.

"You won't?"

He gave her his best bad-boy grin. "No. I'll be using your phone number, instead."

"Oh."

Her face pinkened again, and Garrett's body ignored his brain and went into overdrive. He'd never thought pink a sexy color, but darn if he wasn't curious about what her body would be like naked and all pink from lovemaking, her flesh hot with the sheen of two bodies becoming one.

He inhaled a deep breath, trying to regain some control. Making love wasn't part of his game plan. He didn't need a woman in his life, or a one-night stand, no matter how sexy the counter girl was and no matter how long he'd been without. Cliff could keep his saddles-are-for-riding analogy. One date would get Garrett's life in order and the guys on the force off his back. He gathered his wits.

"I guess we should properly introduce ourselves. I'm Garrett." He put his hand into the slot.

"Olivia," she said. She reached forward and touched his.

The moment their hands connected, a spark shocked him. Wow. Static in July? Her wide, beautiful blue eyes told him that she'd felt the spark, too. He dropped her hand and placed his in the back pocket of his jeans, the safest spot he could think of for the moment.

"Well, Olivia, as pleasant as this has been, I have to get home and feed my cat. He gets cantankerous when he's not fed on time. May I call you so we can arrange our date?"

"Yes." Her voice gave an enchanting squeak and she nodded. She grabbed a blank piece of paper, took a pen and scribbled down her first name and two phone numbers. She held the sheet out to him. "Home and cell," she offered.

"Great. I'll call you soon," Garrett said.

"Okay," she said, now seeming shell-shocked at the turn of events.

He hummed as he exited the *Monitor* office, deliberately leaving the handwritten classified ad behind on the counter.

OLIVIA WATCHED as Garrett moved out of sight. Had he really just asked her out? Had she really propositioned him? Surely this had been some daydream. Some fantasy.

Man, she hadn't even closed her eyes. Would she look like an idiot if she pinched herself?

"So how did it go? Sorry I took so long. I stopped and got some candy. Did he place an ad?"

Chrissy's return reminded Olivia that Garrett's presence hadn't been a daydream, and she snaked her hand forward and snatched the piece of paper that Garrett had left behind. She crumpled it and the ad form and dropped both into the wastebasket before Chrissy saw anything.

Olivia put on her best wistful expression as Chrissy returned to the counter. "He changed his mind."

"Oh." Chrissy sighed wistfully. "The good ones always do." She dug into the file cabinet and brought out a calendar. "So what did he want?"

"Just some information," Olivia answered vaguely. Her religious parents had raised her not to lie, but her PR training let her stretch the truth a little. He had wanted information. Her phone number.

The bad girl could do penance later.

"That's too bad," Chrissy said. "I bet he'd make some woman pretty happy. I mean, look at him."

Olivia glanced at the calendar. Now her PR training failed. There, in full-gloss color, one foot on a police-car bumper, stood her man.

He made Erik Estrada in his *CHIPs* heyday look like a nerd.

Garrett wore his dress uniform and a come-hither smile that could melt chocolate. He dangled handcuffs from his left hand.

"He's the only one not showing any skin, but he doesn't need to, does he?" Chrissy blew out a breath of air. "He's Mr. August, so I can stare at him all next month. And you should see some of the other guys." Chrissy flipped through the pages quickly. "I *had* to buy this calendar—after all, it was for charity."

She held up the photo of another guy, this one a firefighter, bare-chested and wearing suspenders and his firefighting pants. "Twelve months of yum."

Chrissy turned back to Mr. August—Garrett, Olivia thought, remembering his name. He'd be on display for thirty-one days next month.

"He was just as good in person," Chrissy continued. "If I wasn't married I'd let him cuff me anytime. Heck, I'd put 911 on speed-dial if he showed up when I called. Wouldn't you?"

Olivia giggled, her laugh due to from the hysterical combination of having a date with the man and Chrissy's silly behavior. "You're funny."

"Yeah, I know," Chrissy said with a grin. "Some things don't change."

Olivia knew that her friend would never cheat and that her words were all for show. Still, Olivia thought, as she took a final glance at the calendar, Garrett sure did make you aspire to commit a crime. And she had a date with him. One date. One night. If this was what being a bad girl got you, maybe she should have signed up earlier.

Panic suddenly roared in as the full impact of her brash actions hit her. The man was sex personified, whereas she hadn't seduced anyone. He was excitement; she was boring. Exactly what had she gotten herself into?

Chapter Three

"So, did you do it?"

In the middle of opening the refrigerator in the staff lounge the next morning, Garrett stopped. Cold air swirled around him as he checked his watch. He punctuated his words with a low whistle. "Impressive. You waited all of ten minutes before you jumped me."

"What?" Cliff frowned. He leaned against the doorframe.

Garrett retrieved a bottle of cold water, then he shut the refrigerator door. "I said, I was impressed that you waited a full ten minutes to find me once my shift started."

Cliff grinned, his guilt obvious and unabashed. "Yeah, well, I had to stop for coffee. The stuff here is not that good when Cletus brews it, and Tuesday's always his day."

Cliff saluted Garrett with his coffee mug and pried himself from the door frame. He walked over to a red vinyl chair and sat. "And you still haven't answered my question. Did you place the ad?"

Garrett took his time walking to the table. He made a show of opening the plastic water bottle and taking a long sip. Then he set the bottle down, and just to stall for more time, he ran a finger under his collar. Since he was headed into the field, he wore casual clothes: a blue polo shirt and jeans.

Cliff narrowed his eyes, indicating his displeasure at Garrett's stalling. "Should I get Ben and Mason in here? They're dying for information, but I told them that you might be threatened by all of us interrogating you at once."

"Like, that's probable," Garrett said, taking perverse pleasure in Cliff's being antsy. "As if Ben and Mason would intimidate me. You just wanted to be able to spread the news yourself."

"That, too," Cliff admitted with a sly grin. "So?"

"So what?" Someone had left the front-page section of the *St. Louis Post-Dispatch* on the table and Garrett pulled the newspaper toward him. The Cardinals had won again.

As for the deliberate delay, Garrett figured his best friend deserved some grief for his impertinence. That Garrett had lost a poker game and gotten himself into this situation didn't matter; in life post-Brenda, Garrett was a man determined to control his own destiny as much as he could. And that meant making Cliff squirm. Call it part of the guy code.

"Even a few of us against one is intimidating to any man," Cliff said lamely. "They were going to be here, but I stopped them."

Garrett grinned, the image of the counter girl in her silly high-school outfit entering his head. He'd been thinking about her all night.

"But I'm not any man. I'm Garrett Krause, bachelor god. All women want me."

Cliff practically spit out his sip of coffee he started laughing so hard. "Such ego. You're a thirty-six-year-old has-been with only a cat to keep him warm at night. Now, did you place the personal ad or not?"

Garrett couldn't resist. He gripped the edge of the table with both hands, leaned forward and stared Cliff in the eye. "No," he said.

Cliff's reaction was textbook. In the midst of another drink, he muttered and sputtered. His hand shook, sending hot java over the edge of the cup and splattering onto the white table. "Great. Not only did you wimp out, but I could use a paper towel."

"Napkins are over there next to the fridge." Garrett gestured magnanimously with his left hand. False concern laced his voice. "You didn't nail the floor, too, did you? Who knows how often they mop that."

"No, I didn't get the floor. I got me, instead. Not that you'd care about that. Tell me why we're friends?"

"Because we're the only ones who can tolerate each other?" Garrett quipped.

"Ha-ha," Cliff said, but a smirk had crept over his face.

Garrett took a drink of water before holding out the bottle. "Do you need some?"

Cliff set the mug down and began to daub the half-dollar-sized dark spot that had formed on his T-shirt. He accepted the bottle. "Yeah, I need some, or I'll be a leopard all day. That'll make me seem real professional when we go question the victim's neighbors."

"So did he do it?"

Cliff's jaw dropped as some of the other detectives crowded into the doorway. "I told you they weren't going to wait." He turned to the other officers. "What do you think he did?"

"I think he's a chicken," Pete said. At fifty-something, he'd been on the force for over thirty years and married equally as long.

"Even I know how to place a personal ad," Mason said, moving his six-foot-seven frame into the room. He towered over the rest of the men. "Come on, Garrett. How difficult can it be to fill out a simple form? Hell, we fill out paperwork all day. You had to be good at it, or they wouldn't have made you a detective. No one wants to read a cruddy report."

Ben simply stared at Garrett speculatively. "I don't think Garrett's that stupid," he said. "He made a bet. I'm sure he followed through somehow."

Ben was only one year younger than Garrett, but being the youngest didn't always mean slow to catch on, Garrett thought. No wonder Ben had advanced to detective early.

"So what's up your sleeve?" Ben asked.

Garrett made a show of studying his bare arms. "I didn't place the ad," he said.

"You admit you didn't!" Pete slapped his hands

against his thighs. "We had a deal. Boy, you'll pay for this one. My wife even agreed you're lame."

"Moira said that?" Mason asked, his attention on Pete.

"She did," Pete said. "Although, I didn't tell her about the bet. Just that you refuse to date anyone."

Garrett felt his mouth crook upward. Pete's wife sent the guys baked goods weekly. She was everyone's sweetheart. She'd disapprove of the bet.

"Pete, you can tell Moira that I am not lame. The deal was a date. Well, I got that. I will go on one date."

Cliff looked at him in disbelief. "You didn't place the ad. How?"

Garrett kept his face poker still. "The girl behind the counter asked me out."

"You—" Mason stopped himself before the foul language he was about to utter spilled out. "You dog," he said instead.

"That's me," Garrett said, grinning. "All I have to do is call her, go on one date and then everyone gets off my back and leaves me alone. Bet fulfilled."

It was Ben who asked, "Is she cute?"

Garrett paused for a moment and then shrugged. The guys didn't need to know that she'd appeared in several of Garrett's dreams last night, forcing him to take a very cold shower this morning.

"The girl I met is fine," Garrett replied, refusing to describe Olivia in any detail lest she become the subject of gossip. "Besides, it's only one date. That was the deal."

Four faces frowned their disappointment. "One

date," Cliff confirmed. "Yeah, that was the deal. Next time we'll have a Legal Affairs guy sit in on our poker game to make sure the bet's airtight."

"You do that," Garrett said. He retrieved his water bottle, capped it and arched it into the trashcan. "Now, don't we all have work to do? Brainstorm the motives and possible suspects in the Sampson case or something?"

"The guy was missing two years before that dog found his bones. Five more minutes won't matter. When's your date?" Mason asked.

"I haven't set it up yet," Garrett admitted. "I'm supposed to call her."

"Do you have her phone number?" This question came from Ben. "I'd like some verification. Not that I don't trust you, but…"

"I don't trust him," Pete said. "We all know what happens to men who get cornered. Well? Do you have her number, Garrett?"

"Of course I do." Garrett reached into his wallet and pulled out the piece of paper. He handed it to Pete. "Home and cell," he said. "Her name's Olivia."

The men passed the paper around. Ben peered at it longest, then held it up. "This handwriting might be female."

"It is," Garrett said.

He reached for the slip, but Ben stepped back. Then Ben picked up the lounge phone and, before Garrett could stop him, dialed. He held out the receiver to the still-seated Garrett.

"It's ringing," Ben said.

SHE WAS LATE. Olivia drummed her fingers against the leather steering wheel of her Saab convertible. The clock on the dash read 9:05 a.m. Her two-hour weekly workout with her personal trainer had gone over, and she was running a half hour behind. She pulled up at a red light and frowned as a strange noise mingled with the music on her radio.

Her cell phone, resting in the cup holder, was ringing. None of her friends or family ever called her this early. Had they panicked at work already because she was always extremely punctual?

But when she picked up the phone, she didn't recognize the 314 area code glowing on the caller ID display. She pressed talk. "Hello?"

"Is this Olivia?"

The deep baritone voice washing over her sounded oddly familiar, and she worked to place it. "Yes."

There was a brief pause before the sexy voice spoke again. "Hi, Olivia, this is Garrett Krause. We met yesterday afternoon at the *Monitor* classifieds office. Remember?"

Oh, she remembered, all right! Butterflies took flight in Olivia's stomach, and she ignored the car horn blaring behind her. A bad girl didn't care that she was late for work, or that the stoplight telling her to go had turned green. A bad girl cared that the man who'd haunted her dreams last night was actually calling. Olivia had been betting he wouldn't phone, and mentally preparing herself not to be too disappointed. But he had—and the next day, too!

"Garrett, hold on," she said as she dug for the hands-free earpiece she had buried in her purse. She managed to find it and attach the cord to the phone at the precise moment the stoplight turned yellow. She stepped on the gas and waved her apologies to the irritated driver behind her, who was now sitting through another red light.

"Uh, hi," Olivia said, adjusting the thick black cord as she pulled into the lane for the Forest Park Expressway.

His voice was warm and friendly. "Hi, yourself. How are you this morning?"

"Fine." Inwardly she cringed at the lame answer. Come on, inner, bad girl. Don't desert me now.

Another car honked at her, so Olivia put on her blinker and made a quick turn into a Washington University parking lot. Her concentration on driving shot, she idled her car across two spaces. Conversing while parked was safer. The convertible top was down, and a breeze played with the ends of her hair.

"I'm fine, too, even better now that I'm talking to you," he said. Then he gave a little laugh, as if deliberately teasing her. There were murmurs in the background, as though a television was on. "So where are you?" he asked.

"Headed to work," Olivia admitted. "I'm running late."

Although, with him on the phone, she sure didn't care *when* she arrived at the office. With him, she sought to be bad. Very bad. She turned off the radio.

The only sounds now were the hum of the engine and the occasional passing car.

"I don't want to make you late." His bedroom voice sent a shiver through her.

Heck, she'd skip work if he asked her to. "It doesn't matter," she said, putting a pout in her voice. Talking like a seductress was easier when you couldn't see the other person's face. "You told me you work erratic shifts. If you're calling now, this must be a perfect time to talk."

"So are you perfect?"

Far from it, but she wasn't going to tell him that. This man would be her one night, her one digression into forbidden territory. One taste—no more. Giddy with the moment, Olivia let her inner bad girl rule. "I'm perfect in some areas," she said, congratulating herself on how teasing her voice sounded as she answered his question.

"So then tell me one thing," he asked. "How come you're still single? Shouldn't a girl like you have been snatched up by now?"

Olivia's stomach tightened. Though her previous answer had been heavy with innuendo, her words hadn't been a lie. As for her string of failed relationships, she didn't ever intend to tell him the full truth about those. But she hadn't been raised to lie. "I'm still single because I don't settle," Olivia replied, this time making her voice a tad provocative.

She heard his chuckle. "I see."

"Uh-huh," Olivia said. Even though he couldn't see

her, she twirled a piece of her hair coquettishly so that her mood would flow through the phone. "And just so you know, I don't proposition just anyone, either." That was for certain. She'd never propositioned anyone before.

His tone turned serious. "Then I'm honored. So shall we set up our date? I'd like to continue this intriguing conversation in person. Phones just don't work for me. You can't see the person."

Which in this case had been a good idea, Olivia thought. When it came to normal phone conversations with men, she was terrible. Heck, she was terrible with men, period. Her longest relationship had lasted fourteen months, her two engagements each less than that. Garrett Krause wasn't her league. But she only needed one night....

"Let's definitely get this date on the calendar. I'd like to see you again."

"The sooner the better," Garrett said, his sexy tone back.

Olivia's forehead creased, but she reached for her day planner. This bad-girl stuff was new to her. Did all men respond this eagerly? She wasn't sure if she liked it. She pushed her discomfort aside. "I'm ready with my planner now."

"You have a planner?" His voice held surprise. Then he said, "Great. Have you ever been to Melanie's?"

"Melanie's?" She racked her brain but drew a blank.

"I'm sorry. I've never even heard of it. I take it it's good?"

"Despite being just a hole in the wall, Melanie's has some of the best seafood on the South Side. It's on Grand, south of 44, past Tower Grove Park. How about we meet there? Say, Thursday night at six? That's only two nights from now."

Olivia wrote the information in her planner. She circled July twenty-seventh. She couldn't believe that July was almost over. Age thirty-one was getting ever closer. "I'm sure I can find it."

"You can't miss it. The name is on the awning."

She decided she liked his voice. "Melanie's at six," she confirmed.

"It was good talking to you, Olivia. Until Thursday, bye."

And with that, he hung up. Olivia hit the red end button on her cell phone and surveyed the call timer. Less than three minutes. But it didn't matter that she'd never really held a phone conversation with a man for more than ten unless they'd been fighting. What mattered was that she had a date with the sexiest man she'd seen in a long time. "Sorry Sara," Olivia said aloud, as if speaking to her pious stepmother. "But a girl's gotta do what a girl's gotta do. And I have to do this man."

Anticipation shuddered through Olivia. He'd be the ultimate lover. Even though she had zero experience in that area, she just knew he would be. Call it female intuition. Olivia turned up the radio, and humming because Garrett had actually called, she headed to work.

GARRETT PRESSED the off button and set the cordless receiver on the table. He glared at the four men watching him. "Satisfied?"

Cliff grinned, and for a moment Garrett wished he could smack that knowing leer off his friend's face. "More or less."

"I am," Mason said. "You handled that with sheer finesse, buddy boy."

"I don't know," Ben replied, his skepticism obvious.

Garrett stood, glowering at Ben. "Come on, you just heard the whole call. I made silly small talk and asked her out, and she accepted. We have a date on Thursday. Until then I have two different murders to solve and a summer program at Matt's child development center. So enough. It's done. The date's set."

"I'm not saying you didn't ask her," Ben persisted, not at all intimidated by Garrett's solid stance. His green eyes narrowed. "But how do we know that you'll really follow through? That you won't just wimp out, call her back and cancel. Worse, you might stand her up."

"I would never stand her up. That's Mason."

Mason took a step back and raised his hands in protest. "Hey, don't bring that blind date into this. That wasn't funny. I had to run. Did you see her? Murder one ready to happen. I was concerned for my life. Didn't want you guys to have to be rolling yellow tape around me."

Ben flicked his eyes heavenward, then returned his focus to Garrett. "No one's questioning your integrity, Garrett, or your principles. I want to make sure you go on this date. Cliff and Mason date all the time. I'm engaged. Pete's married. But you… If nothing else, I want to see for myself that this woman exists, that she isn't some friend of yours helping you get out of a fix."

Garrett's jaw dropped. "I can't believe you're insinuating I would do something like that."

"No, but I would," Cliff admitted with a grin as he warmed to Ben's current thread. "And you know Mason would."

"Maybe," Mason said slowly. Then he laughed. "Okay, I would."

"So you can understand our concern," Ben added. "Since you didn't place the ad, so we have no real proof of your serious intentions to fulfill the bet, a bet—I might add, that you lost to me."

"I suggest we go along on the date," Cliff suggested. "I agree with Ben. I'd like to see this woman for myself." He paused and glanced over at Ben. "That is what you were thinking, wasn't it?"

"Something along those lines," Ben said.

"Count me out," Pete said. "My wife will kill me. I spend too much time with you guys already. She's starting to harp on me to retire."

"Count me in," Mason said with a shrug of his bony shoulders. "I got nothing to do Thursday night."

"I thought you were hot and heavy with what's-her-name. Did you break-up with the latest one?" Ben asked. "I thought you were getting serious."

"Not anymore. Now we just get together for occasional sex," Mason said. "So I'm free."

"No, you're not," Garrett said. He spoke so forcefully that all the men froze. "This is my date. You are *not* going. None of you. It may have been a while, but I think I can handle a date all by myself. A date is not like a car accident. I don't require witnesses."

Cliff folded his arms across his chest, and at that moment Garrett knew everyone had fully united against him.

"Tagging along is an excellent idea. We'll sit at a table in the corner, have some lobster and crab legs, sip some beer, talk about our current cases—and monitor your progress. We work while you work."

Garrett turned, but his six-foot-three frame failed to intimidate anyone. He needed only one date, and he'd prefer it to be alone. He had principles, for goodness sake. "You all are not going."

Cliff smiled, and Garrett knew before Cliff's next words that he was stuck.

"Yes, we are," Cliff said in a tone that closed the matter. "Now, let's get back to work. As you said, we've got multiple murders to solve."

MELANIE'S was a little storefront establishment that Olivia almost drove by, until at the last moment she saw its name emblazoned on the kelly-green awning.

"Rats!" Olivia flipped on her blinker and ignored the honking from the Cavalier behind her, which had seen better days. *Sorry,* she mouthed to the irritated driver. Luck was with her and she found a convenient parking space on a side street. Steadying her nerves, she parallel-parked her car. The back tire ended up too close to the curb and she was between the lines, but—good enough. As she killed the engine, her phone rang. Thinking it might be Garrett, she answered before she checked the number on the caller ID.

"Olivia," the familiar voice said. The voice of her conscience.

Olivia greeted her stepmother. "Hello, Sara."

"I'm glad I caught you. I heard you left work early the other day. Are you feeling okay?"

"I'm fine," Olivia said. That was the one thing about living at home. Everyone knew your business, even if you had moved out back to the pool house.

"So are you on your way here? I thought you could come up to the house for dinner. Blake's at a meeting and I'm by myself."

Just when was her parents' next stadium tour? For people who were always out saving the world, they'd been home an awful lot lately. Olivia peered in the rearview mirror and checked her lipstick. A touch-up wouldn't hurt. The ravish me red had faded. "I'll have to pass on the invitation. I'm meeting a friend."

"A friend." Sara sounded a tad too bright as she hid her disappointment that Olivia had plans. "Do I know her?"

Olivia groaned. "Actually, Sara, no."

"So someone new?"

"I'm going on a dinner date tonight," Olivia admitted, since the truth was easier than dreaming up some quickie lie.

Sara seemed stunned. "You have a date?"

Without air-conditioning, the car was heating up quickly, Olivia squirmed. "Yes. A date."

"With who?"

"Someone new," Olivia repeated, agitation growing as the car began to bake in the July heat. "We just met. You don't know him."

"Olivia, you're terrible with men. And how can I not know him? I've met everyone in your crowd. You've been hanging out with them for ages."

Which, when one thought about it, was exactly the problem. Olivia drummed her fingers on the steering wheel. One of these days she'd learn to keep her mouth shut. That was what bad girls did.

Bad girls kept secrets from their stepmothers, even if, in Olivia's case, the stepmother had really been the only mother she'd ever known.

Sara considered it her duty to get Olivia married, and to a godly and righteous man. As Olivia's age edged closer to thirty-one, Sara's maternal instinct had grown. What made Sara's constant meddling worse was that Olivia had her grandfather to contend with, as well. He was the ultimate matchmaker.

Grandpa Joe had successfully gotten Olivia's brother, Shane, and her cousins Darci and Harry wed. Figuring that if Grandpa Joe could bring on marital bliss, then she could, too, Sara had turned into a regular dating service for Olivia. The last man she'd introduced Olivia to had aspired to be a missionary deep inside Africa. His plans for their life had driven Olivia crazy after three minutes. No way was she sacrificing running water and electricity to help the less fortunate. Maybe that made her shallow, but not even her parents did that.

A bead of sweat formed on her brow. Time to get going. "Sara, I'm really sorry I can't stop by tonight. I'll come up to the main house for breakfast tomorrow. Give my love to Dad. I've got to run."

Satisfied she'd said enough, Olivia disconnected before Sara launched into the lecture Olivia could tell was coming. Olivia began to put the phone in her purse but on further thought, placed the phone securely in the glove compartment. Knowing Sara, Olivia was sure her stepmother would call back, and nothing was going to ruin this night.

Heck, Olivia's younger half brother, Shane, had sown a bucketful of oats before settling down. If Olivia even mentioned sowing a seed, her stepmother had the whole worldwide constituency out praying for her wayward, virginal stepdaughter. She'd been a fixture in her stepmother's ministry column for years.

Olivia touched up her lipstick and opened the car door. As she stepped out, the St. Louis humidity instantly enveloped her. She smoothed out a wrinkle in her V-necked spaghetti-strap sundress. She'd wrestled all morning with her wardrobe, which had to go from work to her date. How she'd thought about wearing something bad, something black, sexy and oh, so "take me now."

In the end, even if she *had* owned something like

that, she couldn't have done it. Instead, she'd settled for lace underwear, and had worn the sundress for its cleavage-enhancing abilities. She'd left the matching short-sleeved sweater in her office. She gripped her small white purse and began walking toward the restaurant.

As for the date, Olivia couldn't remember ever being so nervous. She'd had enough blind dates in college to last her a lifetime. And then, of course, Sara had paraded eligible men through the endless social engagements that being Blake and Sara Jacobsen entailed. Both types of experiences had taught Olivia that she was terrible on her feet and lousy with idle conversation. She'd learned not to care, to pretend her inadequacies didn't bother her, although deep down they did.

But tonight she worried. None of the men she'd met before had been as sexy as Garrett Krause. None of the men had seemed so ideal.

"Perfect for my project," Olivia told herself aloud, much to the amusement of a passerby. Olivia walked on, voicing her thoughts only in her head. *He'll be my VITO boy.* VITO was an acronym Chrissy had coined in high school—the letters being the first two of the words "virginity to."

He'll be the one I give my virginity to, Olivia thought. *I'm thirty. It's way past time to become a real woman, no matter what my parents say about waiting for marriage and Mr. Right.* Olivia wobbled a little in the two-inch heels she wore. Garrett was tall, and she didn't wish for him to tower over her too much.

Oh, who was she trying to fool? She never wore heels higher than an inch, and trying to be a femme fatale was as foreign to her as going to China. But tonight she hoped Garrett would find her sexy, invigorating, funny and beautiful—and slightly bad. She'd chosen him to deflower her, and she desired all that went along with the kiss and the promise of Mr. Right Now taking her to the edge and beyond. Darn it, she was long overdue. She was tired of reading about it— she wanted action. She was at the restaurant. Her fingers shook as she reached for the door handle. The moment had arrived.

CLIFF WAS ABOUT TO SIGNAL his waitress for another beer, when a movement at the hostess desk caught his attention. He lowered his hand and blinked just to make sure that what he'd seen, he'd seen clearly. He had. What was high-society Olivia Jacobsen doing in a place with zero star ratings, and alone?

Cliff squinted as some sunlight snuck underneath the awning and blinded him for a moment. When he could see again, his mouth immediately dried to a cottony texture. Garrett was greeting Olivia. She had the nerve to blush as Garrett pulled out her chair.

She was five minutes late, but the fact that Cliff had lost the "how late will she be?" bet with the guys wasn't what upset him.

His best friend was about to have a date with Olivia Jacobsen, former fiancée of Cliff's cousin Austin. Cliff's parents had money and connections, but

Austin's had even more. However, the engagement had lasted only four weeks before she'd handed back the flawless diamond solitaire. Less than three months later, Olivia had been sporting another engagement ring, this one more ostentatious than Austin's offering. Of course, that engagement also fizzled. Sure, Austin was now happily married to someone else, but in Cliff's opinion, Olivia had toyed with his cousin's heart.

So what was Olivia doing with Garrett, a man who couldn't afford even a tiny engagement ring since his ex-wife had cleaned him out? This was not good. Garrett had always declared that he'd never date a rich woman again, yet here he was with Olivia. Cliff tossed his napkin on the table. He needed to get Garrett out of here—now. Cliff began to rise to his feet, but sat back down quickly before his partners noticed his erratic behavior.

Cliff clenched his hand to ease the overwhelming tension now consuming him. Had he really been about to confront Olivia? And what would he have said when he got there? He would have acted like a complete idiot. He'd have to trust that Garrett planned on doing what he had said—going on one date and one only.

Cliff frowned. Garrett had called Olivia the counter girl at the *Monitor* office. Everyone knew Olivia Jacobsen was vice president of corporate communications for her family's company, Jacobsen Enterprises. She certainly didn't work behind a counter, but probably in a lush, upper-story office with a fantastic view of downtown. Which meant, could this be a thing staged by Garrett to get the guys off his back?

Cliff took a deep, long pull of the cold beer that the waitress had placed at his elbow. Not only was Cliff a detective with sharp instincts, but he *knew* Garrett. The way Garrett was now toying with Olivia's fingers meant that he didn't have a clue who she really was.

In fact, now Cliff could view almost all of the picture, much the way he did when working a police case or puzzle. Garrett had needed a date to fulfill a bet, and somehow he'd found Olivia, probably at the *Monitor* offices. Why she'd been there was a mystery to solve later. Cliff would bet money that Garrett hadn't asked Olivia her last name. Even if he had, he wouldn't connect some counter girl with one of St. Louis's most powerful families. He had no idea that he was out with a woman wealthier than his ex-wife.

Cliff drained more of his beer, his eyes narrowing as he saw Garrett laugh at something Olivia said. From all appearances, the date was actually going well, and as a friend, Cliff acknowledged he should be elated. Wasn't this exactly what the guys had asked for? That Garrett be back out there on the scene? The deed done, Mason and Ben had already lost interest in Garrett's date and were discussing how they liked the new Busch Stadium, which had opened last April.

Suddenly Ben asked Cliff a question, and Cliff turned his attention away from Garrett and Olivia. He consoled himself with one thing. If she hurt his best friend, Olivia Jacobsen would be dealing with him— and that was a promise.

Chapter Four

Garrett Krause was Mr. Right Now, Olivia decided the moment she'd let him seat her at the table for two. When his fingers had skimmed her bare shoulder, a shiver had ricocheted through her and curled her toes. Whoa.

No man's touch had ever made her react this way. She was alive. Free. And as much as she tried to concentrate on what he was saying, it was impossible when all she could do was watch his full lips move and wonder what they would taste like during a kiss. If Garrett could bottle his sexual magnetism, he could make a fortune.

She'd definitely chosen correctly. Making love to this man would be pure heat. Her two fiancés hadn't even raised her temperature one degree by holding her hand. Garrett's touch had her boiling.

She hoped that tonight that he'd touch her everywhere else.

She attempted to tamp down her desire as the

waitress took Olivia's order for iced tea. Olivia had noticed Garrett drinking the unsweetened beverage, and decided that, despite her desire to be really bad and have some alcoholic courage for the night ahead, being drunk was not the way to accomplish her goal. She had never handled liquor well, and with this man, one drink was liable to have her jumping on Garrett and yelling, "Do me now."

Her desire to lose her virginity to this gorgeous man and thus cross over to the other side and into the womanhood club notwithstanding, climbing all over him was not how Olivia intended to seduce. She wanted the flesh-and-blood act to be wonderful, a thing of which memories were made. She wanted special; she required things on her terms. She'd let parents, religion and morals control her actions for a long time, but that didn't mean she was planning on tossing all integrity aside tonight. Despite her desire to break free, be bad and not conform to the expectations with which she'd been raised, she did not want her first experience to be tawdry.

In the flesh, Garrett Krause was every woman's fantasy, including hers. The red polo shirt he wore failed to conceal the toned body underneath. Golden-blond hair covered his tanned arms. Blue eyes to drown in held her gaze. His full lips had already sent his dimples creasing up toward high cheekbones.

And when his fingers touched her shoulders… Olivia struggled to pay attention to what he was saying and to keep her dangerous thoughts at bay.

"Have any trouble finding the place?" he asked.

"No," Olivia said, grateful for the diversion of his question.

She automatically placed her napkin in her lap as the waitress provided Olivia's iced tea and then refilled Garrett's glass.

"I'll bring you some more crackers, too," she said, and picked up the basket that had more empty wrappers than full packages.

"I'm glad you got here okay," Garrett said. He gestured toward the menu the waitress had left behind. "Shall we decide on some food?"

"That sounds like a plan." Olivia picked up the menu, hiding herself behind it. She began to read the choices, although as Garrett's legs tangled with hers and a heat burned between them, she didn't comprehend one item on the menu.

"Sorry," Garrett said as he moved his leg away.

"No problem," Olivia replied. Yet, it was.

This had to be the most awkward moment of her life, besides maybe her first kiss. After a movie, fourteen-year-old Tommy Hinkins had planted one on her so fast that she'd swallowed her gum and started choking. Her father had performed the Heimlich maneuver, and then during the car ride home given her a biblical lecture on keeping her chastity. Not a very good way to end an evening.

If Olivia didn't do something fast, this one was going to end just as poorly, without her having seduced anyone and reached her goal of becoming a real woman.

She put her menu down, only to find Garrett staring at her.

"What?" she managed to ask.

"Nothing," Garrett said. He grinned sheepishly, his charm washing over her. "Sorry, I just like looking at your eyes. They're unique."

Now, that was a safe topic. "Everyone in my family has them. My grandfather, father and my brothers and sisters, except my stepsister and stepmother."

"Interesting," Garrett said. The waitress deposited a basket of dinner rolls instead of crackers. "The gene for blue eyes is recessive."

Olivia gave a shrug. "I really don't know."

He shook his head, sending a wave of blond hair across his forehead. Olivia popped a piece of Melba toast into her mouth in order to remain poised. He smiled, and it seemed that something molten was running through her veins.

"Sorry," Garrett said again, that grin never changing. "I have to admit I'm a detective at heart, which is why I'm a cop. I love problem solving, so math and science were always my favorite classes."

"I'm not a math person," Olivia replied, filing away that he'd told her his occupation.

"Most people aren't. Let me guess. You were more of an English major."

Olivia nervously touched her hand to the base of her throat as she tried to make a joke. "Does it show?"

Garrett laughed at that, and Olivia began to relax. "Nah. My English teachers never looked like you. If they had, I might have had second thoughts about my career."

Olivia blushed. Okay, maybe she wasn't so terrible at this seduction stuff after all.

Garrett reached for the iced tea in front of him. "So, for a living I solve problems, which in a nutshell tells you all about me. What about you? You work at the *Monitor*."

"I'm in communications," Olivia said. Explaining why she'd been at the newspaper office would take too long.

He studied her for a moment before shooting her a wicked grin. "So you *do* work with words."

"Well, English was my favorite subject. It's what I've always wanted to do. My Barbie dolls were career women in media." She gulped. One step forward, three steps back. To her ears, she'd sounded like a fool. "Great. Now you probably think I'm crazy."

Olivia reached for a roll.

"No," Garrett said. He set the iced-tea glass down and his own blue eyes twinkled. "No more crazy than me. I blew up my G.I. Joe dolls with firecrackers and shot cap pistols at them."

Happiness consumed her. He'd said absolutely the perfect thing to keep her from feeling totally stupid. On other dates, if she had said something like that, the guy would have stared at her, an astonished expression on his face. She relaxed. "You seriously blew them up?"

A muscle in Garrett's cheek twitched and he suppressed a laugh. Olivia resisted the urge to stroke the side of his face.

"I did. Seriously." He held up his hands in a gesture of surrender. "I was just like that kid in *Toy Story*. If I hadn't been a grown man when I saw that movie, it would have given me nightmares for days."

"You were like Sid." She'd watched the movie several times with Bethany's children, Olivia's niece and nephew.

"Yep," Garrett said without apology.

"So," Olivia teased, "tell me. What other bad things did you do?"

FROM UNDER HIS LASHES, Garrett glanced at Olivia. Did she know the effect she was having on him? That dress left way too much to the imagination, and he found himself wanting to tear the cloth off her and see what was underneath. Her skin was smooth, with a natural color that didn't come from tanning. Her smile lit up her whole face and her lips were full and kissable.

She'd be perfect; he knew it as sure as the sun rose in the east. Long pent-up desire that was all he was experiencing, he reassured himself. Just some lust, a normal male emotion. She made him want again. And, that was dangerous. His job required complete control, both mental and physical. Even with volatile Brenda in the mix, he'd mastered both—until tonight.

Olivia folded the menu and placed it on the table. A

part of him tightened as she used those sexy lips to speak. "So, come on. What other bad things did you do?"

"Not too many," Garrett admitted. "My dad was a police officer. So was my grandfather. I always had a fear of being too deviant. They both made sure I saw the inside of a jail very early."

"Scared straight?"

"Yeah, maybe. But I'm determined to bring good to the world and fight evil, all that superhero stuff. Fighting the bad guys is my calling." He paused as a different waitress approached. "Hey, Liz."

"Hey, Garrett," Liz answered. "I'm taking over for Sue. Her boy's sick so she's going home. Are you two ready to order?"

"I think so. Crab legs, Olivia? They're the best in town. Or would you like something else?"

"That sounds perfect," she said. She never had read the menu.

"Bring us both the crab-leg special," Garrett said, handing Liz his menu.

"Coming right up," the waitress said, as she retrieved both menus and walked away.

Garrett glanced quickly around the room. It was bad enough that Cliff, Ben and Mason were twenty-five feet away, laughing about something. Now Liz, Melanie's resident gossip, would fill his partners in on what he and Olivia had ordered.

Olivia took a long sip of iced tea. "You seem to know her well."

Garrett nodded. "A bunch of us often eat here after work. Liz is co-owner. Melanie's her sister."

"Oh. So do you live near here, too?"

"I own a two-family building just west of here. On the other side of Tower Grove Park, just past Southwest."

"I know where that is," Olivia said. "By Favazza's and Cunetto's?"

"Near there," Garrett said at her mention of two restaurants in the Italian section of town Saint Louisans called The Hill. "I live on the second floor and rent out the first to a nice elderly lady. What about you?"

Her face clouded for a moment, as if she was embarrassed. "Ladue," she said, "I rent an unused pool house. The residents are world travelers and aren't home a lot, so I usually have a lot of privacy."

"Ah," Garrett said, although his cop-radar told him something didn't fit. Unlike in St. Louis City, where it was common to see old carriage houses and above-the-garage apartments rented out, Ladue was ritzy and the whole affluent area was known for its huge mansions on three-acre-minimum lots. It was the type of town that would zone against renting garage apartments. Ladue residents were notorious for filing lawsuits over such things as what type of sign you could place in your yard.

But Olivia was smiling, and the things that did to his equilibrium made his cop's suspicions about her place of residence a low priority. After all, he reminded himself, this was just one date.

Liz brought another basketful of bread, this time a different variety from the previous white rolls, and Garrett offered Olivia a piece. "Melanie's runs you through a couple of different breads a night," he said, answering her unanswered question. "Try this. Be sure to use some of the honey butter. It's excellent."

Olivia's fingers connected with his as she took the slice. Heat instantly spread through his body—heat not caused by the warmth of the bread. He definitely reacted to this woman, and again his inner devil stood on his shoulder, whispering exactly what he wanted to do to her.

But Garrett was a gentleman. "Sorry," he said. "I guess the bread's still hot."

"Yes," Olivia agreed as she placed the bread on her plate, buttered the piece and ate a bite. As her lips closed, Garrett tried to stay composed. His only consolation was that her face was flushed, meaning she, too, felt the chemistry.

But this was to be only one date. Just one, designed to impress those guys over there. He would not take her to bed, no matter how tempted he might be.

Their crab legs arrived, and they made small talk while savoring their delicious dinner.

"So," Olivia said as they began to see the bottom of the crab-leg bowl, "what shall we do after this?"

Garrett groaned—the vibration coming from his jeans wasn't desire but his annoying pager. He yanked it out and grimaced as he read the number. Whatever had gone down must be huge for him to be contacted while off duty. Major Case Squad stuff.

"Is something wrong?" Olivia asked.

He hated seeing her expression of concern and confusion, but he didn't have time to explain. He would call en route and find out what was up. "Remember those erratic work shifts I talked about when we met? Well, I've got to go," he said simply. "Something has happened."

Olivia sat stunned, her face mirroring her disbelief. He was tempted to use a finger and smooth away the downturn of her lips. Damn, tonight he'd actually thought of breaking his self-chosen celibacy. He'd planned to at least kiss her goodbye. That would have been nice—feeling the soft touch of some pretty lips.

The page was welcome and unwelcome at the same time.

"You're leaving?" she asked, as if not quite believing he was serious.

"Yes." Garrett stood and tossed a wad of bills down on the table. "That'll cover everything. If not, tell Liz I'll make it up to her next time. I'm sorry about this. I'll call you, okay?"

"Okay," Olivia said, for what else could she say? She watched with acute disappointment as Garrett left the restaurant.

Obviously she wasn't predestined to be a bad girl about to be deflowered. Her stepmother's prayers for divine intervention on Olivia's behalf had probably again been answered. God always was more on Sara's side.

Disappointment made Olivia sigh. Garrett Krause

had been perfect, and making love with him would have been, too. Which meant that unless she wanted to find another male for her bad girl "VITO evening," she had only one option.

She had to wait for Garrett to phone.

Yeah, sure. Did a man *ever* call? Usually when a man said "I'll call you" at the end of a date, especially one he'd left midway through, the words were was a euphemism for "goodbye and good riddance." And math not being her thing, Olivia wondered what the odds were that Garrett would be any different. Probably not great.

So what would a bad girl do now? No answer forthcoming, Olivia glanced at her watch. Just a little after seven. The night was still so young, and now so ruined. She stood up and headed home.

Alone.

HE RARELY WORKED LATE anymore, but tonight Henrietta had a bridge game. Joe Jacobsen, affectionately known to everyone as Grandpa Joe, had always determined that early evening, after everyone had left for the day, was the best time to work.

Joe swiveled his chair to the left, taking a moment to survey the hundred-and-eighty-degree view he had of downtown St. Louis and the Gateway Arch. Two walls of floor-to-ceiling windows gave him a view down Market Street, and the view never failed to satisfy. From his perch twenty-five stories high, he could see Union Station, the Soldier's Memorial and the Old Courthouse far beyond. The slant of the seven o'clock sun illuminated the western face of the metal arch, making it glitter in a multitude of blues, pinks, and whites.

Joe sighed. This was his city and he loved it here. St. Louis tradition ran deep and was often slow to change—a perfect example being the "new" Busch Stadium. Oh, people had fussed over the idea of losing the old stadium in 2005, but once they entered the new one, they fell in love again.

Change was good for the soul. He'd been changing for almost eighty years.

Joe's brow creased, and he absently stroked the beard that often made children say he looked like a thin version of Santa Claus. He was worried about Olivia.

Olivia—sweet, kind and gentle Olivia—wasn't managing change well anymore. She'd dealt with turning thirty last year by throwing herself into her work. She'd earned the position of vice president of corporate communications and had excelled at her job these past eight months. But suddenly, with her thirty-first birthday coming—September fifteen, a little over a month away—Joe's granddaughter was showing changes that he didn't necessarily like. She seemed bored. Anxious.

Of course Joe knew what the problem was. Love. With two broken engagements under her belt, Olivia was more than once bitten, twice shy. She was tired. Olivia didn't have her elder sister Claire's workaholic commitment to Henrietta's Restaurant—a job that kept

Claire too busy even to consider a relationship. Olivia worked a forty-hour week, did some charity work and tolerated her stepmother's matchmaking. And everyone around her appeared suddenly to be settled. Her younger brother Shane was married with a baby. Her cousins had children. Her stepsister Bethany's children were almost ten.

Even Olivia's fraternal twin, Nick, who'd been holed up in Chicago forever, had discovered he loved Maxie, his childhood neighbor-from-hell who'd taken up residence in the condo above his. Maxie and Nick, seemingly two complete opposites, had suddenly dropped the blinders and fallen madly in love. They'd told Joe during his last visit to Chicago, and the two lovebirds planned to tell the rest of the family in a few months, around Thanksgiving.

Joe didn't expect Olivia to handle the news well. Oh, she'd be happy that Nick was headed to the altar, but the result would be that Sara would soon apply double pressure to get the "spinster" Olivia married off.

Sara considered Olivia hers—she'd become Olivia's stepmother when Olivia had been five. The two were often oil and water. Sara was reserved, proper, the perfect person to stand by Blake Jacobsen's side as he ministered to the world. Blake loved Sara without question. But Olivia had her Greek mother Kristina's fire. That Mediterranean passion inside Olivia had been tamped down for years. She'd denied that part of herself, trying to fit into a world that wasn't hers to fit into.

She'd settled into her role as the "perfect one" in the family, becoming the good girl who never failed to meet her parents' expectations. Except in one. Love.

Oh, she'd tried. But luckily she'd come to her senses and backed out before being married to the wrong man just because being married was something she should have achieved by now.

Joe swiveled his chair around and glanced over at the huge grandfather clock his family had given him for his birthday. He'd promised not to meddle, promised not to matchmake. But maybe he could run interference. Give Olivia some space to loosen up, to discover herself. She needed to rebel a little, to break away from her family. She was not going to find her Mr. Right anywhere in the Blake and Sara Jacobsen dynamic.

He'd heard that Olivia had ditched work the other day, and that was a start. Sometimes having a little devil inside you was a good thing. That little devil made you appreciate all the good things so much more, made you recognize the blessings.

As the wheels in his head began to turn, Grandpa Joe smiled. He knew exactly what to do.

Chapter Five

Regret should be a four-letter word, Olivia decided at nine-thirty that night. She could think of a whole bunch of foul words to utter about now, all of which would make Olivia momentarily feel better about the failed result of her bad-girl ambition. Of course, any good sensation gained from cursing would last only until her righteous upbringing kicked in, making her regret saying the curse words, as well.

So much for being a bad girl. Her attempt had been pathetic, and the night hadn't turned out the way she'd planned at all. At this moment, she wasn't losing her virginity to some sexy stud; she was moping, wondering if Garrett had really had a page at all.

Olivia blew out a long breath, turning her focus to making a wayward piece of damp black hair dance. That diversion quickly irked her, and she let the offending strand drop to the left side of her nose before pushing it back behind her ear.

Even punishing her body with a five-mile outdoor

jog, hadn't released the pent-up tension consuming her. The subsequent swim hadn't removed any emotional angst, either. And she hadn't come to any resolution about what to do next.

She reached for the glass of water on the table near her and took a drink. She wore only a towel; she'd stripped off her clothes and dropped them on the concrete when she'd jumped into the pool. It wasn't as if anyone would see her in the dark. High landscaping surrounded the naturally colored pool that sat in the middle of the five-acre estate. The main house was about seventy feet away, just beyond the rose gardens. Swimming naked—alone—was about as sexual as Olivia ever got.

Which indeed made her pathetic—although she had tried to remedy that tonight. Yet now that all was said and done she was glad she hadn't. She'd been prepared to lose her virginity to a man she'd met once. Well, twice. Aside from his name and the fact that he was a cop, she knew nothing about him.

Tonight at the restaurant had been magical—the chemistry fully there. Nature would have taken its course, and she did know all about the mechanics of the act from books. However, how did one ask a man to wear a condom? And did one just get up and leave when everything was done? What would be her emotional state after her first time?

Her father had always preached that the moment was more than chemistry, that lovemaking should cement a bond of two becoming one. The experience her father described was the real reason Olivia had waited all these years. She longed for that perfect moment. But now, as she neared thirty-one, she'd given up on finding the man to make that moment happen in the context of marriage. Unlike those romance novels she loved so much, she'd settle for Mr. Right Now. And until his pager had gone off, that had been Garrett Krause.

Olivia had been prepared to feast on Garrett. But, as with eating chocolate, which tasted great going down, there were always repercussions. Garrett might not leave extra weight on her hips, but deep down Olivia was the kind of girl that having a one-night stand would weigh on. She'd been raised to believe that casual sex was wrong, and that one couldn't just go sin and wipe one's actions away with a quick prayer of "forgive me."

Olivia's conscience was her best friend and her worst enemy.

She sighed in another weak attempt to relieve her frustration. For such a strong, successful career woman, she was a failure at this part of her life. She was no more a bad girl than her stepmother Sara was. Olivia wasn't a romance-novel heroine who could tame a bad boy without breaking a nail. Olivia was a good girl who needed a good man.

Unfortunately those men bored her to tears.

One might think that after two failed engagements she would have learned to be content with what she had, would stop dreaming that real men were like the ones she read about in steamy novels. But she refused to give up or settle. She desired some raw passion. She desired drama. She craved passion.

Why were the good men all boring? Somewhere out there had to be a good man who *wasn't* boring, *wasn't* tepid to the touch, *wasn't* a mouse who tiptoed around her, *wasn't* with her only because of who her parents were or because she had a huge trust fund that could put him on easy street.

Of course, Garrett Krause had not been boring or a mouse or a gold digger. He'd been hot, sexy, charming and, even better, easy to talk to. He'd made her smile, made her laugh and left her with a happy sensation— and all without even knowing her last name.

Yet the night had been a bust, and probably for the best. After all, he'd come to place his ad because he needed only one date. He wasn't looking for a lifetime commitment, which was what she wanted ultimately. Perhaps she should be grateful she hadn't been stuck with the check.

Frustrated at the futility of the evening, Olivia pounded her fist on the chaise lounge's arm. She had to stop thinking about him. He'd left in the middle of their date, almost as if the pager had been timed.

Yet fate's manipulation of Olivia's life had always been that way. Divine intervention, perhaps. God answering Sara's prayers to keep her stepdaughter chaste and pure for some boring, upright man who would give Olivia two-point-five kids, a two-story house and membership in the correct church and country club.

For once Olivia wished she could have what she wanted, which was an exciting, sexy, yet appropriate man for her.

Olivia finished drinking her water, stood, gathered her belongings and went inside. Brightness instantly assaulted her eyes, and she took a moment to blink as she became accustomed to the white light.

Like always, the two-thousand-square-foot pool house was clean and neat. The living area dominated most of the house—when the building, built thirty-five years ago, had been designed to host a large number of people. Olivia never had more than five at a time in the cavernous space that held an antique pool table, several seating arrangements, a huge plasma-screen television and a dining area that could easily accommodate sixteen.

Some designer had long ago furnished the estate, which had been Olivia's paternal grandparents' before they moved farther west and gave their former residence to Blake and Kristina as a present on the birth of their twins.

All the Jacobsens had extensive trust funds, and her younger half brother, Shane, had done some updating when he lived in the pool house. Beyond the kitchen designed for entertaining lay three bedrooms. Shane had used one for his office and one for his assistant Lindy's office, and had kept the master bedroom for himself. He'd married Lindy and moved out, and when Olivia moved in, she'd added the plasma TV and a few other touches. She'd redone the master bedroom, commandeered Lindy's former office as hers and left the other bedroom empty. It wasn't as if anyone ever stayed over.

Olivia put the water glass in the dishwasher and went to take a shower. She'd redone the ensuite bathroom, changing the colors to robin's egg blue and crisp white. Being in the master bedroom suite was like being at a beachside retreat in the Virgin Islands. Tonight the irony of the "virgin" decor wasn't lost on Olivia, and after her shower she changed into silk tap pants and a camisole, an outfit that sounded sexier than it was. She climbed into bed and turned on the ten o'clock news. The top story was about the discovery of two bodies near the Meramec River in Castlewood State Park.

"Major Case Squad investigators arrived on the scene just after seven-thirty tonight," the reporter said, the camera's spotlight harsh on her face. Behind her a yellow strand of police tape was visible, but the rest of the scene was bathed in darkness. "Investigators are calling this a double homicide, as it appears the bodies had been weighted down. Our dry spell has lowered the river level, and the bodies got caught on a boat's propeller as the fishermen were returning to the ramp. No one at this time will estimate how long the bodies had been in the water."

"Gross," Olivia said as she flipped the channel to a cable show. She watched that for a few more minutes, then turned off the TV, double checked both her alarm clock and the alarm she always set on her cell phone and switched off the light.

Her cell phone's shrill woke her up a little while later. The clock on the phone showed it was after eleven, and the caller ID displayed only a number, not a preprogrammed name. As head of Jacobsen communications, she knew she could get phoned at any hour if something significant had to be dealt with, such as a major PR issue. "Hello."

"You were sleeping. It's too late. I shouldn't have called."

The moment the baritone voice reached through the earpiece Olivia clicked on the nightstand light and sat up. "Garrett?"

He didn't confirm but said, "I'll call you tomorrow. Go back to sleep."

"I was awake," Olivia lied. He'd phoned, and the adrenaline rushing through her meant she wasn't letting him off the hook easily. "My light's still on. What's up?"

There was a moment of hesitation. "I wanted to apologize. This is the first free moment I've had since I left and it's bothered me that I had to run out on you right in the middle of dinner like that. We'd hardly finished the entree."

"You told me you have erratic shifts," Olivia said. She clutched her cell phone. "You told me you're a cop. I figured something happened."

"It did. Besides my duties for my local police force, I'm an investigator with the Major Case Squad. A fisherman found two bodies in Castlewood State Park and we were assigned to handle the case. I'm finally on my way home, and honestly, I wouldn't have gotten a good night's sleep if I hadn't apologized to you. Running out like that—that's not how I am. I hate leaving the wrong impression."

As she heard his words, a giddy sensation tickled her, banishing any vestiges of sleepiness. He'd called. He hadn't lied to her or made anything up. He hadn't simply ditched her. Maybe the night was salvageable, although not in the way she'd wished for it to end earlier, when she'd selfishly desired only to lose her virginity. Now that the night had waned, the bad girl was gone, replaced with a girl who was extremely curious to find out more about this man. He was a good man who wasn't boring. That made him rare.

"I really appreciate your calling me. I did see a story on the news," Olivia said. "I didn't know that you were involved."

"We volunteer, but only some of us get selected. Our home force lends us to the Major Case Squad if the case is in our jurisdiction as this one is. Anyway, if you saw the story, then you have as much information as we do. We've divided up the work, broken up into teams, and since I was off duty when the body was found, I can go home and snag some rest. Some guys will be working through the night. I go back at eight a.m. tomorrow. After that, I doubt I'll get much sleep for the next week."

No sleep? "So where are you now?" The words jumped out of her mouth as if of their own accord.

"I'm just about to hit the 44 and 270 interchange."

So he wasn't to the St. Louis city limits yet but still in Southwest County. "Are you hungry?" she asked.

"A bit," he admitted. "I didn't really get to finish dinner. Crab legs aren't that filling, so I was planning to stop and grab some fast food on the way home."

"Why don't you turn north on 270 and come up here and I'll cook you something. Like I said, I'm awake, and a bit hungry, too. This way you won't have to eat alone."

The idea had merit, Olivia thought, the moment after she'd made the offer. Despite having eaten earlier, she *was* hungry. An intense run did that to a person.

He seemed hesitant. "You're offering to cook me something? I was just going to drive through a—"

"No fast food," Olivia said quickly before he could shoot down her idea. "You'll probably be eating that nonstop once the case get going."

"Most likely," Garrett admitted with a laugh. "That part of the stereotype is true."

"So come up here," Olivia cajoled. "I've already got some chicken thawed and it's pretty easy to toss meat on the grill. I don't live far and my place is easy to find."

"You're sure?" He sounded hesitant.

"Positive." Olivia said firmly.

"Okay, I'm on the northbound ramp now. How far up 270?"

"You'll get off at Ladue Road," she said, and then, much to her delight, they made conversation about random things during the next twenty-five minutes as she directed Garrett to her house.

"Turn in the small service drive about one hundred fifty feet beyond the main drive."

"I see it."

"I'm in the pool house. Once in the service driveway you can't miss the pool house. Here come your headlights. I'm hanging up."

"Okay."

Olivia disconnected and glanced down at her clothing. She'd been so caught up in their conversation that she'd forgotten she was wearing only a cami and tap pants. She made for her closet, but Garrett was already knocking at the back door. She couldn't leave him standing there. What she was wearing would have to do. Besides, her lingerie wasn't anywhere close to indecent—many high school girls paraded about the mall in less. She tamped down her nervousness and went to open the door.

OLIVIA LIVED HERE? Garrett's shoes crunched on the expensive pea-gravel-and-stepping-stone walkway. No regular concrete sidewalk led to the door. Rather, the rock path meandered through professional landscaping and ended at the biggest pool house he'd ever seen. The dwelling dwarfed many starter homes.

Garrett raised his hand to knock on the side door but paused. Just what was he doing here? He'd parked his American compact car behind a convertible Saab. The six-year-old Malibu had shuddered as the engine sputtered and died, perhaps intimidated by the high-performance machine sitting inches off its bumper. And could someone explain just how a counter girl drove a Saab? Things just weren't adding up, and disquiet stole over him.

Sure, he'd wanted to see Olivia and where she lived, but he still questioned himself about why. An apology for running out on dinner should have been enough. Why had he said yes to her offer to cook? And when he'd turned onto Upper Ladue Road, with its million-dollar houses, he'd entered a world that he'd left behind three years ago.

Although, even Brenda's parents hadn't been as wealthy as the people who owned this entire property must be. That hadn't stopped Brenda, who'd insisted that she could drive nothing less than a Lexus SUV. His ex-wife had had three priorities: luxury, shopping and status. St. Louis was a city defined by where you went to high school and, later, what country club you joined. Garrett, who'd attended Lindbergh High School in South County, hadn't been privately educated. He had been decidedly middle class. His parents hadn't spent fifteen thousand dollars a year or more to cover tuition at a private high school. He'd gotten a full scholarship to the University of Missouri-St. Louis, graduated, and entered the police academy.

His marriage to Brenda remained one of his life's big mistakes. He'd met her through Cliff, and the chemistry between Garrett and Brenda had been immediate and intense. But intense chemistry was like a match—a quick flare and a fast burn that left nothing but useless ash.

Garrett had learned; he knew better than to trust

chemistry. His work as a Major Case Squad investigator had also taught him to distrust any emotion that existed on the extreme. Passionate emotions could cause rational people to do the most irrational things. How many times had he seen crimes of passion in his work? Many of the murders he solved would never have happened under normal circumstances. But when emotions flared… People did things they never would do.

Was that why he was about to knock on Olivia's door? Heck, he didn't even know her last name. And nothing about this woman made sense—not her car, not her job, not her house, not her—

"Hi," she said as she opened the door.

At that moment Garrett knew how a moth approaching a light must feel. Excited. Elated. Despite the danger. Instead of a mature man of thirty-six, Garrett found himself feeling like a schoolboy on his first date.

"Hi," he said, his gaze roving over Olivia. Her face devoid of makeup, she appeared younger and prettier than she had earlier that evening. Her black hair danced over her shoulders, and his fingers itched to roll a strand between his thumb and forefinger.

"Come on in," she said. "I didn't have time to change, so if you don't mind, let me first get you something to drink and then…"

"You're fine," he said, the words catching in his throat as he followed her into the kitchen area of the house. He found he didn't want her out of his sight. "Don't change on my account unless you really want to."

Olivia stood there in her yellow cami top. His cop's training observed the one-inch straps that would easily conceal a bra if she were wearing one. The scooped neckline was three inches above her cleavage, and the matching yellow tap pants provided full coverage of her slim body. The outfit wasn't designed to seduce— a swimsuit revealed more—but by its innocence, her clothing was having just that effect. "Okay."

Olivia was a paradox, and he was fast discovering that he didn't care if he understood why she was or not. So much for his determination to avoid raw passion. Saying something and doing it were two different things. Olivia pressed a cola into his hand, the ice-cold aluminum reinforcing how much chemistry was in the room. So much for avoidance. He was very aware of this woman.

"I'm sorry I don't have any beer. I don't usually keep alcohol in the house," she replied, her expression apologetic.

"Soda is fine," Garrett said. He remembered that she'd had iced tea at dinner, too. "I'll be driving soon, anyway, and when I'm driving I don't drink. I see too many DWI cases."

"Okay," she said. She opened the refrigerator and removed a plate of boneless chicken breasts. Garrett popped the top on the soda can and took a draught as Olivia began to take spices out of the cabinet. She added them to the meat, put the meat in a plastic storage bag and returned the contents to the fridge. Then she disposed of the chicken packaging and wiped down the counter with a disinfecting wipe.

"I hope you aren't going to too much trouble," he said.

She glanced over. Amazing what power her smile held.

"Not at all. I love to cook. My family's in the restaurant business so I learned how at an early age. Trust me, you'll be amazed at what I can scrounge up on short notice. I've got some sugar snap peas and some rice already steamed."

"Impressive," he said.

She laughed at his compliment. "Not really. While I did promise you a home-cooked meal, I have to admit that the rice is left over from last night. But once I heat it up and add some spices, you'll never notice. At least, I hope you won't. Follow me. I have to light the grill."

Garrett trailed her out into the living area and gave a low whistle as his gaze swept over the room. "I like the pool table. Is all this yours?"

"I rent it," she said. "The interior decor came with the house. Like I said, the owners are rarely in town and they hardly ever use the pool, and they haven't used the pool house for years. Their son lived here until he got married, and after he moved out, it became available and I moved in."

She opened a pair of French doors and they went out to a huge patio. There she flipped a switch, making dozens of hidden lights glow. Then she led him by a huge built-in gas grill, the kind that costs at least five thousand dollars. The patio itself appeared to be professionally designed: teak seating pieces surrounded a huge concrete pool that blended seamlessly into the ground foliage. The private tropical-resort theme succeeded fully.

"This is very nice," he said. Small, lit fountains in the pool had begun to bubble, audibly creating the illusion of a trickling brook.

"I know—I'm lucky," she said. "I come out here all the time and relax. The hot tub's just out of sight around that corner, and there are two outdoor changing rooms in that small building over there. Whoever designed this place thought of everything."

"It's great," he acknowledged, a tad envious. The rich really did live differently.

She started the grill and closed the lid. "My favorite spot to sit is over here. Come on. You can tell me more about yourself—well, if you're game."

"There's nothing more to tell," he said as he followed her to a spot nestled in a bend of the pool. As they settled onto two chaise lounges, he noticed the quietness of the night. In the city, the endless traffic drowned out the sounds of nature. Here he could hear crickets.

"Surely there's something to tell," Olivia prodded. "I read your ad. You mentioned loving kids and cats."

He nodded. This vein of conversation was safe. "I have one cat. I only put that in the ad since someone said I'd eliminate the cat haters that way. Narrow down my choices. As for the rest of my bio, I'm divorced," Garrett said. "It was final over three years ago. I have a son who'll turn five in October."

"Do you get to see him a lot? I'm sorry. That was probably prying." Yet Garrett could see nothing but understanding in her eyes. Her interest in his life was genuine. She was not digging for information so much as trying to understand him.

"I don't see him as much as I'd like to," Garrett admitted, finding talking to Olivia easy. He rarely shared personal things with anyone but good friends, but he felt comfortable opening up to her. He worried about revealing himself to her for a moment, then dismissed his concern. "Matt means the world to me. The divorce wasn't very pleasant."

"I'm sorry," she said. "I can't really say I understand, but I don't have a good romance track record, either. I ended two engagements, and that wasn't easy. I cared for the men, but not really anything beyond friendship. I was in relationships for the wrong reasons. Still, seeing them end is like watching a dream die."

"Exactly," Garrett said. She had grasped what he meant. They sat there in silence, listening to the trickling of the water.

"So did you grow up knowing you wanted to be a cop?" she asked, breaking the silence.

"Yeah," he said. "My dad and grandfather were cops, so I guess you could say police work is in my blood. I'm the first investigator, though, and the first one in my family to get a master's degree in criminal justice." He answered her unspoken question. "I went to UMSL."

"Did I read somewhere that their program is one of the top five in the nation?"

"You probably did. It's true." he said, and as he spoke, more of his earlier tension drained away. Garrett didn't have a private college background, but in his field, most of the top schools were state-funded. Olivia, sitting in her very expensive environment, didn't seem to care about his profession, or his less-than-wealthy background. She seemed to just like him.

Olivia used the moment to rise to her feet, her dark hair dancing over her shoulders. "I'm going to get the chicken. I'll be back in a few minutes. Don't hesitate to explore, so long as you don't go up that path over there. It leads to the main house, and the owners are home this week. They're usually in bed by ten."

"Okay." He watched her disappear into the pool house before rising to his feet. Curiosity prompted him to explore the changing room, where he found swimsuits of all sizes in addition to dozens of perfectly folded towels. He located the hot tub, a freestanding eight-person model inset into a custom redwood deck. The cover was on, protecting the water from the elements.

"It's ready if you'd like to get in. The top retracts via that button on the wall," Olivia said from behind him.

He turned and saw that she carried a plate of chicken.

"Maybe another time," he said as he stepped away. "Can I do anything?"

"Nah. I've become a grill expert," she told him. "I learned once I moved in here."

Olivia tossed the chicken onto the grill and the meat sizzled.

"So, besides living here, what else about you don't I know?" Garrett asked.

"Nothing, really. Deep down I'm a boring person," she said as he approached the sink. She squirted some soap into the outdoor sink and washed the plate. "I'm Ms. Non-excitement."

He saw she was serious. "That can't be possible."

"It is. I go to work. I come home. I do a little volunteer work. I try to please my parents. I'm a pretty down-to-earth person. My ideal night is movies and pizza."

"Then I'm probably also boring," Garrett said. "I do pretty much the same thing, though I don't volunteer for anything."

"You probably don't have time with your work shifts. Anyhow, your job has to be exciting." Olivia rinsed the plate and let it air-dry.

"There's a lot of paperwork and chasing down endless leads. A lot of reaching dead ends and starting over. Seriously, *Cold Case* and *CSI* make crime solving sound thrilling, but in reality it's nothing like what you see on TV. I also don't handle every Major Case Squad file, and I have duties in my home police department."

"That must keep you busy," she said. She flipped the chicken over, and again the grill sizzled.

For the first time he noticed that her feet were bare and that she'd painted her toes with a vivid red polish. How had he missed that? Even in the soft background light of the patio, he could see the way the polish contrasted with her skin's natural glow. He swallowed hard.

They continued to talk, until Olivia announced "Dinner's done" and began to transfer the chicken back to the clean plate. She faced him. "Do you prefer to eat outside or in?"

"In," Garrett said. Being in the indoor light might give him some much-needed perspective. Here, in the gentle glow of the terrace, he was finding it difficult to resist this woman. Something about her drew him. He didn't need this complication in his life, but he was discovering he minded less and less. Maybe because she made him feel alive again, feel that there was life post-Brenda and post-Mr. August.

Inside, Olivia served him dinner at the kitchen bar. Garrett took a seat on the stool and found that the dinner she'd prepared didn't disappoint. She'd steamed the sugar snap peas, and they were perfectly crisp and flavored with a hint of spice. Summer savory, she told him. The flavored rice might have been left over, but he couldn't tell. And the chicken with its a delightful flavor of cumin and peppers melted in his mouth.

"This is delicious," he said as he lifted another bite into his mouth. "*Much* better than fast food. Thank you for cooking for me."

"You're welcome," Olivia said.

HE'D DEVOURED her food. What a special night this had turned out to be. She and Garrett were like two magnets, Olivia thought. When by themselves, the magnets didn't do much but their job. But when put together they could attract or repel, and oh, when they attracted…

She was definitely attracted to Garrett. It had happened quickly, and she found herself wanting more. She fancied herself spending another night with him, and then another, maybe doing that movie-and-pizza thing. As he set his knife and fork down, she wondered what to say. How did you tell a man who'd started out needing only one date that the woman who'd only needed one night, wanted to turn that one into several, and really get to know him?

Maybe you just said the words—but as Garrett stood, carried his plate to the kitchen and rinsed the plate before placing the dish in the sink, Olivia found herself mute, her earlier courage in issuing the dinner invitation gone.

"There's more soda in the fridge," she said.

"Thanks." He opened the refrigerator door.

She gawked as he bent over and retrieved a can from the bottom shelf. The man should be outlawed from wearing jeans. He shut the door, leaned against the counter, popped the top and took a long drink. "Dinner was great. Thanks again."

"No problem. I'm glad you stopped by. I had a really good time tonight."

"Then I'm glad everything worked out the way it

did," Garrett said. He strode across the kitchen. He was three feet across the breakfast bar from her, the countertop a protective barrier. "I certainly didn't expect our dinner at Melanie's to be interrupted so crazily."

"Tonight's been a grand adventure," she said. "A bit like a roller-coaster ride. I told you, my life's boring. It could use a little livening up."

"I'll never believe that," he said. He placed his elbows on the counter, the soda forgotten. "You have to be the most intriguing woman I've ever met."

"Is that good or bad?" she asked, her mouth puckering.

"I'm really not sure," he said, his eyes unblinking as his gaze held hers.

"Ah." She pushed her stool back and planted her feet on the floor. Across the room a grandfather clock chimed one a.m. "It's late," she said, grateful for the interruption. She was out of her league here. This man was worldly. He had done things she couldn't even imagine.

"And I bet you have to be at work early." He straightened to his full height.

"Always," she said. Her life was methodical, preordained. She existed in a protective bubble. Outside it was another life, and once that bubble broke, she couldn't fix it. Like Pandora's box, once opened, everything would be irreparably changed. Earlier, that was all she'd wanted. Now, she realized the full implications of her decision. If Garrett kissed her, life would never be the same.

GARRETT WALKED AROUND the breakfast bar and entered Olivia's space. A contradiction within her had just reared its head. Just as on the day they'd met, he had seen her insecurity. She had been nervous, although she'd covered her expression quickly, but he'd noticed the conflicting emotions, intimating she wasn't the brash female who'd first propositioned him at the *Monitor* office. Her hand shook slightly, almost imperceptibly. But he was a cop.

Despite all the mysteries swirling around Olivia, his gut instinct told him she was genuine. Maybe he could let his guard down just a little, if only for this one moment. She turned, those blue eyes with their outer rim of dark blue widening. Her lips parted. The next step was his, probably a step he shouldn't take. Passion and chemistry led down the wrong path. They came to naught. His marriage proved that.

But at this time—tonight—he needed. The part of him he'd denied since Brenda's betrayal yearned to know that he still could be liked just for himself, by the right woman.

If she existed.

He had to find out. Garrett leaned down and captured Olivia's lips.

Chapter Six

Whoa! As Garrett's lips touched hers, Olivia panicked. Kissing wasn't something she could…

Do.

Never mind. As Garrett continued to kiss her, the panic passed. And as his lips worked their magic, the question haunting her found an answer.

What did a bad girl do? The same thing that a good girl did. What came naturally.

Olivia heard herself give a little cry as Garrett deepened the kiss. There was nothing tepid about this man. His right hand had snaked into her hair and his left arm had circled her waist to bring her closer. For Olivia, the moment was a revelation. She wasn't frigid; she could be passionate. His lips teased and nipped hers, trapping her bottom lip in a soft suckle before letting go. His tongue traced her flesh and Olivia's mouth parted further allowing him to slip inside.

The gesture sent a shiver through her, for the first time in her life. Her mind wasn't on her shopping list, or on the fact that she would be tired tomorrow at work. Under Garrett's ministrations she could concentrate only on desire. Romance novels had it right. When the perfect man kissed you, the earth did move, time seemed to stop and you simply became one with sensation.

His mouth tasted of soda, yet nothing had ever tasted so divine. Her hands against the red polo shirt he wore, her fingertips splayed against the solid chest beneath. The endless kiss sent her spiraling, and pressed against him the way she was, she could feel the part of him that strained beneath his tight jeans. She was making him hard. And instead of being unresponsive as she had been with her fiancés, she found herself wanting to use every one of her five senses to explore this man.

She'd been correct. He was Mr. Right, the man for her. Not for just now but for beyond, as well. That thought flitted in and out of her consciousness as he used a finger to trace her jaw.

"You are intoxicating," he whispered as he planted kisses on her cheeks and her eyelids. "You're doing things to me."

"Bad things," Olivia said.

"Never," he said.

Olivia's eyelids fluttered open and she saw his intense expression.

"Never," he repeated. And then he groaned and brought his lips back down to hers.

Olivia reveled in his passionate kiss. Almost of their

own accord, her hands tugged his shirt up and slid underneath so that she could touch him without barriers. His skin was smooth under her fingertips, his chest hairless. Her fingers moved farther, tracing his nipples and exploring his pectorals, which seemed larger than her hands.

He'd slid his hand beneath her camisole and now stroked the skin of her lower back. She'd waited a lifetime for a touch like his. The clock chimed the half hour and Olivia ignored the annoying sound.

But suddenly Garrett drew back, his gaze searching hers. She knew he was getting ready to end the evening.

"This is…"

"Right," Olivia said simply as the newfound woman took over.

"Right," he repeated before she took charge and captured his lips with hers.

She wasn't ready to stop. Just a little more. That would be okay…

This time *she* kissed *him*, and, while doing so, led him over to the couch. She sat next to him, and his hands moved to her breasts, cupping her first through the fabric, then sliding underneath it to rub her between his thumb and forefinger. Her legs tightened and her head rested back against the upholstery. Garrett's lips sought the place his fingers had been.

To be suckled and lathed was heaven on earth, Olivia decided, before the thought vanished and the pleasure she was experiencing overrode rationality again.

"I didn't intend to seduce you," she whispered.

"I know," he said. "We should stop."

Her entire body shook from the sensation of his re-instated kisses. "Don't stop," she said. "Not yet."

"I will when you tell me," he said, and Olivia let her head fall lower onto a decorative throw pillow as the cami top vanished and his fingers moved to discover the crevice between her legs.

She was so wet, and his fingers found the slickness and rubbed it over her and into her, sending her into orgasm.

"You're driving me crazy," he told her as her pants went the way of her top. He replaced his fingers with his tongue and drove her into oblivion again.

"Olivia," he said, his lips against her legs. "What do you want?"

"Everything," she said. She'd come this far, and she would not be denied now, could not in this moment that was so perfect. He guided her body so that she lay on the couch, and she was glad for the lights as he pulled off his shirt, then his jeans, and then his plaid boxers, revealing a man who stood ready.

As she touched him, he groaned. She'd seen the calendar picture but not the actual flesh, and now she cupped her hand and ran her palm up and down his shaft. A drop formed on the end and she circled his tip with her thumb. Growling he yanked himself from her grip. He bent, that tight rear end in prime view as he grabbed his jeans, removed his wallet and retrieved a condom. Then he ripped it open, drew it over him and settled himself between her legs. Her left leg slipped off the couch, and then he was at her entrance and pressing through.

Oh. Two becoming one. The pain. The pleasure. The delight. He stilled, but she lifted her left leg and wrapped it around his lower back. Her hands moved to the sides of his thighs.

"Are you okay?" he murmured in her ear.

"Absolutely," Olivia said as her body adjusted to his presence inside her. How could she not be? Never in her imagination had she dreamed lovemaking would feel like this.

He began to move, slowly at first and then picking up the pace as he drove himself into her. Passion took over, and the beginning of her first internal orgasm began to build. Beads of sweat fell from his forehead to hers, and as he leaned down to kiss her, she and he seemed to breathe as one. She raised her head and watched his thrusts, just once, before she leaned back into the pillow and her body raced to fulfillment. She couldn't help but cry out as her body shook.

She could sense when he found his release, for his face became something magical. Then he lay on top of her, still joined, and she was secure in his arms as he planted kisses on her face.

"You okay?" he asked again.

"Wonderful," Olivia said as he ebbed inside her.

"I didn't intend for this to happen when I said yes to dinner," he murmured.

"I know," she said. His face was so close to hers,

his breath warm on her cheek. "I didn't intend this when I asked you over."

She touched the sides of his face, the stubble prickly beneath her palms. A trace of guilt stole over her. She *had* planned on this happening before he'd run out on the dinner at Melanie's, but then she'd tossed the idea aside. She hadn't expected this when she invited him over.

He slowly disengaged himself from her. "Bathroom?"

"First door down the hall," she said.

He grabbed his clothes and strode off, unabashed that he crossed her living room totally naked. Olivia moved herself to a sitting position and slowly began to dress. She hadn't had any bleeding, but since she was an avid horsewoman, that wasn't surprising. She was, however, sore. She pulled on her clothes and waited.

The few minutes until Garrett's return felt like an eternity. The grandfather clock ticked off the seconds, the only sound in the huge room, and Olivia sat there wondering what would happen next.

Her answer arrived when he returned from the bathroom, took her hand and assisted her to her feet. Then he kissed her. Long and intense.

"I've got to go, and you should get some rest," he said as he lifted his lips from hers.

"Probably," she admitted, trying to find her footing on this shaky new ground.

He kissed the tip of her nose. "Thanks for dinner

and a great evening. I'll call you this weekend if I get a free moment. The case is going to make my life crazy. Sometimes I work twenty-four hours straight before getting any rest."

"Okay."

She followed him to the door. Once there he kissed her quickly, and then he was gone, his headlights making a wide sweep as he backed out of the driveway.

Olivia stood unmoving in the open doorway for several minutes. Finally she motivated herself to step outside. She double checked that the grill was off. She flipped light switches, sending the patio into darkness. Then she went back inside where she turned off interior lights on her way to her bedroom. Pausing at the foot of her bed, she contemplated his parting words. He had said he would call.

He'd done so once.

Would he do so again? Or had this been just one night—the one night she'd originally thought she could settle for? Her parents said the devil worked like that—setting you up for a fall by giving you what you wanted once you'd changed your mind.

Olivia exhaled a long pent-up breath. For a moment she'd been as close to Garrett as a woman could be to a man. And now she was alone, but the degree of being alone had intensified. It was like having traveled to the best place you'd ever been, and not knowing if you'd ever get to return. "Wanting" and "longing" had magnified.

She had to resign herself to the fact this was

probably a one-night stand. As the passion and the adrenaline of the evening faded, Olivia climbed into bed and drew her comforter up to her chin. Doubts danced in her head. It would be a restless night.

OLIVIA SLEPT UNTIL TEN the next day. She woke once around seven, decided she didn't care to see anyone and phoned in sick to work. Then she rolled back onto her stomach, buried her head under the covers and slept another three hours. Sleeping somehow made last night fade a little—at least when sleeping, she didn't think of Garrett and what she'd done.

Besides, the idea of still being in your pajamas instead of behind a desk had merit, she decided later as she padded her way into the kitchen to make some coffee. She'd never played hooky from work for a full day before, but she now had a three-day weekend.

Although, most of the day was already booked. She had her parents' dinner party tonight and a family event to attend tomorrow night. As her hand hovered over the coffee can she frowned. Was that someone at the door? She squirted across the breakfast bar and grimaced as she recognized the figure standing at the patio door.

It might be after ten, but it was still too early. Olivia held up a finger to indicate "wait a moment," added the coffee grounds to the filter, started the machine and then went to admit her stepmother.

"Good morning," Olivia said as Sara stepped through the French doors.

"I thought you were coming up to the house for breakfast," Sara said. Her gaze roved over Olivia in a nanosecond assessment. "When it was obvious you'd forgotten, I dialed your cell. That went directly to your voice mail, so I called work. They said you were sick."

"I just got up," Olivia said. With Garrett's arrival last night, Olivia had forgotten all about promising to meet Sara for breakfast.

But obviously her stepmother had been awake for hours. At fifty-six, Sara Jacobsen had a full head of white hair, cut in a bob that barely covered her ears. Since Blake had a private trust fund, Sara could afford to shop designer, but she had instead mastered the art of discount chic. Claiming that everything required fitting, she was an accomplished seamstress who altered all her clothes before she wore them. Thus, her clothes always graced her slim figure. She was a tall woman, although age had knocked an inch off her five-foot-ten frame. Olivia had known her stepmother for twenty-five years, and she really didn't remember Sara any way except determined. The woman had not walked down here in the summer heat just to socialize.

"It was nice of you to drop by," Olivia said, trying to kick-start the conversation.

"I have a luncheon at the Junior League, but I knew I must drop by and see how you were doing. What's wrong? Allergies? Summer cold?"

"I'm just tired," Olivia said with a yawn that wasn't faked. "It was a long night."

Sara nodded. "I noticed that. There were lights on

down here until two a.m." Sara's voice held an under-current of rebuke. "Your father had a live interview at midnight our time. It was morning in Germany."

"Oh, a German television show?" Olivia's father was always doing things like that.

"Yes," Sara confirmed. "I also noticed a car behind yours."

Olivia sighed. The one night her parents stayed up late… "I had a friend over. I cooked, and I think I gave myself food poisoning. I was up most of the night."

Sara's eyebrows arched and her lips puckered. "You never were much of a liar, Olivia. You've always had a face that's as transparent as glass, especially to me. I thought you had a dinner date last night. So did you cook for him? Or after dinner bring him back here?"

Olivia clenched her hands counted to ten and released them. How had Shane lived in this pool house and managed his playboy lifestyle? Was it because Olivia was female that she was being held to a higher standard, which meant an inquisition? Already despondent over the uncertainty of her relationship with Garrett, Olivia was riled no end at the thought that Sara would treat her differently. She was an adult and perhaps it was time to remind her stepmother of that.

"Sara, whatever I did is none of your business. I'm a grown woman and I deserve some privacy."

"So you *did* something?" Sara seemed stricken. "Olivia, you aren't like your brothers. You don't have the temperament for—"

Olivia stomped her foot. It did little good, but the

childish movement gave her some way to vent years of frustration. "You have no idea what I have the temperament for, Sara. I am almost thirty-one and I have lived my whole life to your exacting standards. Well, that stops now. A man can come back to my place for coffee and dinner, because I am of age to have him do so. Your lack of trust and faith in me is pretty pathetic."

"Olivia, your father and I only want to see you happy. We want you to find the right man. And sex outside of marriage is not the way to contentment or commitment."

"Who said we had sex?" Olivia shot back, but her body betrayed her. She felt a telltale flush stole cross her cheeks. So this was what it was like to have known carnal desire. Parts of her had heated as if trying to relive Garrett's touch.

"Dear God," Sara said. Her brown eyes narrowed. "You did, didn't you?"

"So what?" Olivia shrugged, her anger at herself and what she'd done with Garrett finding a convenient outlet by targeting Sara. "I was tired of being the perfect virgin you flaunted in your ministry column. He made me feel alive. Cherished. Much more so than any of those dull men you keep trying to foist off on me as appropriate husband material."

As Sara's eyes widened in shock, Olivia found herself unable to stop the vile things that spewed from her mouth. She'd never spoken to Sara like this. Being bad didn't taste good, and deep down Olivia knew she'd regret her actions later, but for now, bitterness about her previous behavior ruled.

"I'm going to live my life my way, Sara. Maybe I'll find someone. Maybe I won't. But I'm tired of waiting, and I'm tired of doing everything deemed right and proper by someone else's definition."

"Olivia, it's God's definition."

Olivia raised her hand, like a crossing guard motioning stop. "My life, Sara. Let me deal with God, okay? You and my father have raised me, but at some point you have to leave me to find my own path. I am capable of doing that."

"Olivia, you—we—" Sara simply stopped. She pursed her lips as the patio door clicked open.

"I'm not interrupting anything, am I? I came to see the patient." Grandpa Joe stood there, casually dressed as if he'd been out playing nine holes instead of going to the office.

Olivia blinked. Was everyone taking Friday off?

"Hello, Joe." Sara gave her father-in-law a kiss on the cheek as he entered the room. "You aren't interrupting. I was just about to leave for my lunch at the Junior League. Olivia, you will be there tonight, won't you?"

"Yes," Olivia said, her earlier defiance ebbing. She'd rather avoid tonight's dinner party, but the event was important to her father's ministry, and she'd promised. Hopefully Sara wouldn't parade too many eligible men by her. There was only one Olivia wanted, although whether he wanted her was open for debate.

"I'll see you at five-thirty, then." With that, Sara left and strode back up the path to the main house.

"I heard you were sick," Grandpa Joe said. The Jacobsen blue eyes twinkled. "Playing hooky, are we?"

"Not you, too." Olivia sighed. "Do you mind if I get a cup of coffee before you start in on me, as well?"

Grandpa Joe chuckled, his beard shaking a little. "Only if you also get me a cup. As for starting in with you, my only thoughts are that it's about darn time."

Olivia leaned back studying her grandfather as he sat down on a stool at the breakfast bar. "What?"

"Your attendance record is a little too exemplary for a girl your age. You should be out having fun, not hanging around the office, winning every attendance award."

"Is it so impossible for everyone to believe I was sick?" Olivia said as she poured hot java into two mugs.

Grandpa Joe stroked his beard. "You've inherited my healthy genes. I'm never sick, either. Take off work without having scheduled your absence weeks in advance, and everyone panics. Now, if you're ill a little more often, people don't worry as much. It's normal. They accept it more readily."

"I see," Olivia said. When she took a sip, the hot coffee burned her tongue and she swallowed quickly. She set the mug down so the contents could cool. "I guess that makes sense. Be careful—the coffee's really hot. So were you worried, or is there another reason for this trip?"

"You always were the clever one of the group. Caught me. I've been worried about you for a while, but not because you live at the office. You just haven't seemed happy lately, and I figured today was as good a day as any to solve a mystery and cheer you up. So, yes, I have an ulterior motive."

Her spine stiffened. "Sara just called me transparent. Does everyone think I'm a loser who needs a pep talk?"

Grandpa Joe shook his head, and his fingers tapped the side of the cup. "I'm not even going to dignify that with a response. But, Olivia, you have been living your life on everyone else's terms, and I'm concerned. You need to be out doing what's best for you. Especially with the announcement coming up."

"What announcement?" Olivia asked.

Grandpa Joe held her gaze. "The one that your twin brother's getting married."

"What?" Olivia stared at her grandfather. If she'd had coffee in her mouth, she would have spewed it everywhere, so great was her shock. "Nick?"

Grandpa Joe nodded. He was dead serious. "It's a secret. I'm the only one who knows. He told me in confidence when I was in Chicago last."

Olivia tried to steady herself. "He can't be getting married. He wasn't dating anyone."

Grandpa Joe's eyes showed his empathy. "He's marrying Maxie."

"Maxie? Maxine Gildehaus? They're complete opposites. She's an artist, always flaunting her latest conquest. Nick's a lawyer and wears a bow tie like Linus Larrabee in *Sabrina*." Olivia leaned against the kitchen counter for support. "Nick and Maxie?"

"They've known each other since childhood. Why do you think I insisted she get a condo in Nick's building? Eventually I knew he'd wake up and see what was under his nose. That's what Shane had to do with Lindy. It took him three years and some strawberry daiquiris to get a clue."

Olivia closed her eyes for a moment, seeking temporary refuge in the brief darkness. She opened her eyes. Grandpa Joe's expression hadn't changed. "I can't believe Nick didn't at least tell me they were dating. We always used to tell each other everything." Of course, that was before Nick moved to Chicago. Except for their weekly e-mails, they had drifted apart as confidants.

Grandpa Joe's expression was sympathetic. "I think he's worried that it'll make you feel like an old maid."

Trust her grandfather to put the truth out on a platter for all to see. "I'm about to turn thirty-one, not sixty-one. That's not an old maid. Why is it that a woman has to be married in order to be deemed successful and fulfilled? I have a great job, my volunteer work and all my stepmother's unsuccessful matchmaking to contend with. Life is full."

"Olivia," Grandpa Joe chided gently. "I've known you since the day you were born. I was the third family member to hold you. You have your mother's Greek heritage. You are passionate. You've been denying that innate zest since she died. Now, I love Sara, but she's cloistered you and subdued your natural spirit. You haven't lived. You're so wrapped up in being godly that you've lost any sense of being worldly. I love this town, but St. Louis is very structured and rigid. Your parents overshadow you. You need to break out, be free and soar. Be who you want to be."

Olivia sighed and drank her coffee. Aside from her twin, her grandfather had always been the one family member she could confide in. He was the dad she'd wished for, one who could spare the time to teach her golf and tennis and not just turn her over to a pro. Grandpa Joe was the one to set business aside and take her fishing. He'd been the one to send her to camps that weren't always Bible-based. Olivia never had blamed her father—after all, Blake Jacobsen belonged to the world. He had a higher calling—that of bringing men to Christ.

"You always have an ace up your sleeve," Olivia said. "What are you suggesting? Where are you going with this?"

"Well, I did overhear part of the conversation you had with Sara—that there's a man in your life who could change things. But I was thinking that you might like the position that is about to open up."

The career woman inside her perked up. Whereas parts of her life had occasionally been bumpy, her career path had been smooth. She might be incompetent at some things, such as men, but she was good at her job. "What position?"

"The last time I was in New York to check on Jacobsen's Manhattan restaurant, Cameron O'Brien and I got to talking. O'Brien Publications is expanding again, and will be hiring a vice president of communications. We were thinking you might be an excellent fit."

"Me?" Olivia squeaked. O'Brien Publications was a media conglomerate that was gaining fast on Rupert Murdoch's empire. To be considered for a position at O'Brien Publications was flattering.

"You." Grandpa Joe nodded. "It's a new job, and it won't begin until the end of October. It would require your relocating to New York City, but Darci's there and she could help you get settled and find someplace decent to live. And you met Cameron's sister Kit at Darci's wedding. She and her husband have offered to help out in any way, as well."

"Wow!" Olivia said. Delight had her giving a little shake. "That's quite an offer."

"It's a huge career leap from your job at Jacobsen Enterprises, that's for sure," Grandpa Joe said. He paused and drank some coffee. "Mull it over for a while. The announcement making the position official won't take place until late September, so you have plenty of time. Once it's official, if you're interested, call Cameron and discuss it with him."

"I will consider it. Thanks." Funny how when one door closed, another one opened. New York City. She'd seen every episode of *Sex and the City*. New York teemed with life, and perhaps that's just what she needed. A chance to break free. Nick had escaped to Chicago. Darci had moved to the Big Apple. Maybe it was time for Olivia to fly the coop, as well.

Long after Grandpa Joe had left and Olivia had showered and changed, she walked over to the couch where she and Garrett had made love. *No, had sex*, Olivia corrected herself as she adjusted the decorative pillow on which she'd placed her head. She had to be practical and acknowledge last night for what it was. She'd lost her virginity to a one-night stand. At least she'd proved to herself one thing—that she could be passionate. She'd have to be satisfied that that was enough.

FIVE O'CLOCK FRIDAY afternoon found Garrett eating a foot-long roast beef sub and drinking a twenty-ounce cola while finishing up his lead sheet.

The way the Major Case Squad worked was simple. Comprising of members of various police departments from the forty-five hundred square miles it served, officers of the squad, when called out, were still paid their salaries by their home forces; officers were considered "on loan" to the requesting agency for the duration of the investigation.

The idea behind the Major Case Squad was that if area police departments pooled resources and worked together, they could solve the most heinous crimes. Since its inception in 1965, the squad had conducted over three hundred fifty-five investigations at the request of eighty-three Missouri and Illinois police and sheriff's agencies. It had successfully solved approximately eighty-one percent of its cases.

To become a member, Garrett had first had to have his own police force recommend him; then he'd had to submit a résumé. The squad selected only the best officers, and Garrett was proud to be a part of the group. Donations and contributions funded the squad, and it was a shining example of police department cooperation.

After reporting for duty at the command center at eight, Garrett had been assigned lead number seven to follow. The case had drawn twenty-six men from police forces surrounding the crime scene. To foster cooperation, the men were divided into teams of two, partnering with someone from outside their home force. Garrett had been assigned a partner from the Ballwin Police Department.

Today, Garrett and his partner had phone duty, and after that, lead seven to follow up on. Garrett hadn't been part of the intensive site investigation that morning. Not that site investigation was Garrett's specialty. His was interviewing witnesses. The task of searching for clues in nature better belonged to others. Those officers had found scraps of fabric attached to briars about a half mile away in the woods, along a little-used hiking path.

The scraps had been sent to the lab to see if they matched the few pieces of clothing left on the bodies. Except for some remnants, the bodies had been naked, and the investigators had to determine whether the water had removed the clothes or the bodies had been stripped by the murderer before being tossed in the water. The medical examiner would confirm whether the men had been dead before being weighed down, which the Major Case Squad had already determined was the likeliest scenario. Stripped, killed and dumped into the river to rot. Garrett winced. He loved his job, but sometimes the sights weren't so pleasant.

The command center was busy, and Garrett's partner returned with some fresh coffee. "Here," Garrett told him as he passed over the folder on lead seven. It had been a dead end. "This report is done."

"Great. I'll get the next lead. Ready to go back out?"

"Always," Garrett said. Often the Major Case Squad could track leads for weeks and come up with nothing. Other times they got lucky immediately. Overall, the squad had a "some of this might be is promising" attitude.

"You look tired."

"Oh, hey Cliff," Garrett said. A police department could send anywhere from one to three people, and Cliff had been called in this morning to work at the command post. He'd been assigned a partner from the state highway patrol. "I am tired," Garrett admitted. By the time he'd gotten home and climbed in bed, he'd had only three hours before his alarm went off. "What lead do you have?"

"Twenty-nine. Before I go exhaust this one, tell me, how was your date?"

Now wasn't the time or place for this conversation, especially not after what had happened later that night at Olivia's house. So Garrett answered with a vague "You saw how it went. You were there, remember?"

Cliff grinned for a split second before sobering. "Yeah, and you left her in the middle of dinner."

"Occupational hazard," Garrett said, finding himself irritated. He wasn't planning to talk about Olivia, especially not after three hours of dreams that had made his sleep less than refreshing. "I fulfilled the bet. Don't tell me you're going to say that because I got paged I have to go out again."

Cliff shook his head, the earlier grin gone. "No. You're done. I don't think she's a good candidate for you, anyway."

Garrett leaned back in his chair, the murder case forgotten for a moment. Cliff looked serious. Considering the intimacies he and Olivia had shared, Garrett wanted to know what Cliff was getting at. "What do you mean by that? You didn't even meet her."

"No, but I'm an investigator, and I just thought she was a little too…fake."

And Cliff had determined this from twenty feet away? "I didn't," Garrett said. He'd made love to her, for goodness sake.

"You said she worked at the *Mound City Monitor?* But those were real pearls," Cliff pointed out.

"So?" Garrett shot back, now even more agitated. Cliff was bringing up some things that Garrett himself had wondered about, and had dismissed when passion carried him away. He, who understood firsthand all about how dangerous passion could be, had found himself slaking lust on the first date. Still, he was honor bound to defend Olivia. "Maybe her parents gave them to her."

"Which reminds me, did you ask anything about her family?"

"Why does that matter?" Garrett said, his anger reaching a boiling point. He didn't need Cliff to remind him how little he knew Olivia in some areas, and how well he knew her in others. Garrett knew what sound she made as she climaxed; he knew how her lips puckered as she reached a new peak. Yep, ardor and hormones had erased all his normal level-headedness last night. Garrett had broken his vow to be celibate. While he liked Olivia and had enjoyed the evening, he wasn't necessarily proud of what had transpired. He'd tossed aside all restraint.

And now Cliff, without being privy to why his words were having an impact, was reinforcing how out of character Garrett's actions had been. "Garrett, you're a cop. You can't go on dates with women you don't know. You're lucky the pager went off and you could end the night then."

Garrett knew the best way to get Cliff to back off was to go on the offensive. "Why this sudden change of heart? You were all over me to go out with her. What is it?"

Cliff gestured with his hands. "I just worry that you'll do something rash. That's how you got Brenda, and no one, especially me, wants to see you get hurt again. Back out there, yes, but probably with someone who has a little more life than a counter girl at a classified ad department."

"I had a good time with her," Garrett said, skipping over the fact that he already had done something rash. He'd made love to her and damn if he didn't want to go right this moment and do it again.

"Garrett, you should have a good time with a bunch of women," Cliff said. "Not settle for the first one you find."

"First one? Barely a year ago women were crawling all over the station. I could have had any of them, no strings attached. I'm not that kind of guy. There had to be something about Olivia that made me ask her out."

"Yeah. A bet. A way not to lose face with the guys. I'm your best friend, Garrett. Level with me. You only went out with her so that you could get everyone off your back. Admit the truth."

"That was it," Garrett said, just so Cliff would stop bothering him. After all, that was how things had started. "But I did have a good time," he added stubbornly.

And to make it anything less cheapened the evening, and what had happened later. Garrett suspected Olivia wasn't the one-night-stand type. She hadn't even been very experienced, and that had been refreshing. He'd discovered something special with her, something beyond simply having ended his celibacy.

"Just take your time," Cliff said.

"Oh, don't worry, I doubt that with this case I'll have much time to see her again."

"That's probably a good thing. She didn't strike me as right for you."

Garrett rolled his eyes. She'd been *very* right. Right underneath him, right when she'd kissed him, right when she'd let him slip away without a scene. He'd promised to call her. He wasn't the type of guy who broke those types of promises.

The return of Garrett's partner interrupted the conversation. "Garrett, we've got lead thirty-nine. You'll like this one. A caller asked if the clothing was off the bodies when they were found and described one of the fabric patterns. I called her, and she's agreed to meet us at the Daniel Boone Library in an hour. She's afraid she's being watched."

"Let's go," Garrett said, his problem with Olivia and what to do with her relegated to a back burner. He had a case to solve.

As GARRETT STOOD to leave, raw relief calmed Cliff. When on a case, his buddy Garrett was singularly focused. That trait was one of the things that had driven Brenda crazy. Garrett was tenacious, and he wouldn't let go of work until he saw justice served.

Perhaps this case was just what Garrett needed. In Cliff's opinion, the last thing Garrett should do was go on another date with Olivia, a woman who hadn't revealed who she was.

And the last thing Cliff wanted to do was confront Garrett on how rich Olivia and her family were. Let the man have his illusion of Olivia the counter girl.

After Brenda and all her lies, protecting Garrett by leaving him his fantasy—so long as that was all it was—would be fine. After all, Garrett would soon become focused on the murders, and by the time he remembered he should have called Olivia, it would be too late to do so without coming across like a complete fool.

Everyone knew that if a guy didn't call within five days after he said he would, then he'd just meant the words as a polite goodbye.

If necessary, once back in their home police department, the guys would talk Garrett out of calling, anyway, and then the problem of Olivia, and whatever agenda she had, would be solved.

Case closed.

Chapter Seven

"Hey, Garrett. Welcome back."

"Thanks," Garrett said as he walked toward his desk. Two weeks had passed since he'd been assigned to what the media had dubbed the Meramec River Murders, and with two suspects now under arrest and one singing like a jaybird, the squad had been pared down to four officers. This had sent Garrett back to his regular police job in the Bureau of Crimes Against Persons.

It was already Monday, August fourteenth. After the arrests, Garrett had taken a few days' leave to spend time with his son before Matt started his new school. The little guy had one more year before kindergarten, but he'd been accepted at the prestigious Rossman School, their junior kindergarten. The school was inordinately expensive, but Brenda's parents had agreed to pick up the fifteen-thousand-dollar tuition tab.

"Hi, Garrett," Audra said. She served as administrative assistant to the detective staff. "Wunderlich asked that you stop by his office."

"Did he say why?" Lieutenant Wayne Wunderlich was Garrett's commanding officer. He'd been with the force almost twenty years.

"Nope," Audra said. "Just that you should see him as soon as you arrived."

"Okay," Garrett said and he detoured down a short hall, to the offices with exterior views. He rapped on a door, and the lieutenant glanced up.

"Garrett, great to have you back. You cracked that case wide-open," Wunderlich said as he waved Garrett inside.

"My partner and I just had a hot lead sheet. We interviewed the girlfriend of one of the victims. She didn't believe her boyfriend had dumped her, and her suspicions were justified. It all boiled down to arguments over methamphetamine."

"I hate meth. Damn stuff causes more problems… Anyway, good work. Reason I've called you in here is that I haven't gotten your RSVP for the barbecue and Trisha's hounding me." Trisha was Wunderlich's wife.

"Barbecue? Oh, the annual division barbecue."

"Exactly. Our bureau is in charge of this year's shindig and Trisha is overseeing the RSVPs. It's this Saturday at Queeny Park. We've practically taken over the place. Anyhow, I told her three. You, your son and a date."

"I don't know about the date, sir," Garrett said, shifting his weight.

"Oh, bring someone," Wunderlich said. "Ben mentioned you were seeing someone."

"Well, I…" Garrett began.

"Bring her," Wunderlich insisted. "As Trisha says, the more the merrier. We'll see you Saturday."

With that, Garrett knew he was dismissed. He headed back to his desk to catch up on the paperwork that had piled high in his absence.

Cliff's desk was across from his, Pete's, a few rows over. Mason and Ben were on another floor.

"So what'd he want?" Cliff asked.

"My RSVP for Saturday," Garrett said. "Ben told him I'm seeing someone, so Wunderlich told me he put me down for three."

"Gotta love Ben," Cliff said, sarcasm obvious. "Always trying to help. RSVP numbers don't matter. You can just show up with Matt. No one will remember or care."

"I know," Garrett said. Besides, he was used to going places solo, or towing just Matt.

But not this time.

Eighteen days had elapsed since he'd seen Olivia, and the stricken expression on her face as he'd left the pool house still haunted him. He was a heel for leaving her the way he did.

She probably thought he'd used her for a one-night stand. Garrett had meant to call her, and he had reached for his phone several times. But then the case would get busy. Or Matt would call. Or something else would come up. As days passed, Garrett figured he should have forgotten her. But for some reason, he couldn't. She had gotten under his skin.

He had to undo a wrong—call her and apologize, even if he made a total fool of himself. Of course, maybe she'd forgive him, as she had previously. Her flame had singed him, but he wasn't burned. Instead of being put off by her secrets, he found himself intrigued. But he had promised to call and hadn't. He had to accept that she might not want to see him. Rejection was a risk. Still, amends first, another date afterward if possible. The moment Cliff went to lunch, Garrett planned to pick up the phone and dial.

HER CELL PHONE was ringing. No one ever called her on it during work, and of course, the one time she'd forgotten to turn off the ringer, the phone had to shrill, right during a meeting in her office. Now everyone was staring at her, expressions curious.

"Sorry." She barely glanced at the caller ID as she pressed the button to send the call to her voice mail and turned her attention back to finishing the presentation. "Lisette, show me those new brochure ideas and then we'll break for lunch. I'm sure everyone is hungry."

Twenty minutes later Olivia checked her phone and frowned. She didn't recognize the number. Probably a misdial; she'd been getting a lot of those the past two or so weeks. The screen popped up, indicating she had voice mail. Olivia pressed the key to connect.

She almost dropped the phone when she heard the voice. "Hi, Olivia. It's Garrett. I'm a cad—I fully admit it. When I'm on a case I become totally focused, and I didn't do what I said I'd do, which was call. Please accept my apology. If you're still willing to talk to me, my cell number is 314-555-2191. My direct line at work is…"

Olivia grabbed for a pen, and ended up listening to the message two more times as Garrett finally provided his home, cell and work phone numbers. He'd even told her he'd be at work until four that day.

Should she call? She leaned back in her office chair and drummed her fingers on her desk. Instantly annoyed with the staccato noise she was creating, she swiveled around to gaze out the window and stare down Market Street.

She'd had two weeks to contemplate what had happened between Garrett and her. Losing her virginity had given her a new perspective on men, and on relationships in general. She understood now why people easily lost themselves in the pleasures of the flesh. She understood why her father preached that such an intimate act should only occur within the context of marriage, where stability was assured.

Worse, another effect of her and Garrett's lovemaking was that Olivia had gained visual reference for those steamy novels she read. No longer was she just imagining the act. She had made love, which had made one thing clear: she required love, attention and the passion that flared between two people. She wanted happily ever after.

Instead, her life was now topsy-turvy. Not only had she received a lecture from her mother the morning after her initiation into womanhood, but that evening during the dinner party her mother had introduced Olivia to at least three more eligible men. Although Sara had redoubled her efforts, there had been zero interest on Olivia's end. Sure, they were appropriate, nice men. But Olivia was fixated on the one who'd gotten away—the one who'd left her sitting on the couch with a promise to call.

And now he had. Over two weeks later.

She could at least phone him back and hear what he had to say. That didn't commit her to anything. Maybe he meant what he'd said on her voice mail. That he was sorry. The bad girl whispered that she should call, but Olivia banished the bad girl to the back of her mind. Being bad had gotten her into this fix in the first place.

"Hey, Olivia, I didn't expect to catch you. Must be my lucky day."

The male voice and a rap on the door had Olivia turning and rising as her younger brother entered her office. "Shane. I haven't seen you in days. What's up?"

"I wish I were here on a social call, but I could use your help. I've got to give a talk at a Kiwanis Club luncheon later this week and you know how terrible I am at writing speeches. Think you could help me?"

"Of course I can. Come in. Tell me, how're Lindy and Bradley?"

Shane's face softened as Olivia mentioned his wife and eight-month-old son. "They're fine. I admit it, I'm jealous. I'm so used to seeing her all the time, but ever since she decided to stay home after Bradley's birth and she no longer works here, I miss her during the day."

"You did work side-by-side for three years," Olivia said.

"Yeah." He pushed a strand of blond hair away from his face. He was Blake and Sara's son, and the only feature he shared with his half sister was his Jacobsen blue eyes. "So do you think you can help me? I'd use Franz, but he's on vacation this week."

"Of course I can," Olivia said, in truth a bit glad for the diversion. "Tell me about the subject and some of your ideas, and let's see what I can think of."

"Great," Shane said as he settled into a wingback chair in front of Olivia's desk. "I'm not keeping you from lunch, am I?"

She shook her head. "No. I had a bagel during the meeting, so I'll scavenge something later when I'm hungry. There's plenty of time, no one's due back until one. What's the speech on?"

Shane explained for a few minutes until Olivia decided she had all the information she needed. "That should do it. I can have this done for you by tomorrow afternoon. I'm working on the new ad campaign today for Jacobsen's. We did the video yesterday, and today we're finishing the print."

"I couldn't be that creative," Shane said. "So how's life in the pool house? I didn't get a chance to talk to you much the other weekend during our fun-filled family event. Is Mom leaving you alone?"

"For the most part."

"Which means she's still being a matchmaker from hell. I'm glad those days are over for me, although she simply ropes Lindy and me into other things, instead. This weekend she's got something else going. I managed to worm my way out."

Olivia contemplated that for a moment. "Maybe that's what she called me about today. She left a message on my voice mail. I was going to call her later."

Shane grinned. "Well, beforehand, you better find something to do. Whatever her event, she'll find a way to matchmake."

"Probably," Olivia agreed. "She seems to have an endless supply of them."

Shane rose to his feet. "You take care, sis, and I'll see you late tomorrow. Will four work to pick up the speech?"

"Four is fine," Olivia said. Shane was almost to the door when Olivia said, "Hey, Shane. I've got a question. If a guy calls a girl two weeks after a date and says he's sorry he didn't call earlier, should she call him back?"

The corners of Shane's mouth lifted. "Does the girl like him?"

"Perhaps just a little," Olivia admitted. "On his message he did say that he was busy with work. He's part of the Major Case Squad. He was working those Meramec River Murders."

Shane nodded once. "Then he probably was busy.

And a cop usually wouldn't lie about phoning women— not given the level he's at in the force. Those were pretty grisly murders. Call him, Livvy."

"Maybe," she said.

Shane's smile lit up the room. "So he's a cop. Boy, won't Sara just love that? And a homicide detective to boot."

"Out," Olivia ordered, pointing of her forefinger. "See you tomorrow. And please, if you don't mind, shut the door behind you."

Brotherly smirk still in place, Shane saluted her, then turned and left, closing the door. Before she could talk herself out of calling, Olivia reached for the phone.

"GARRETT KRAUSE."

"Hi, Garrett. This is Olivia Jacobsen. I'm returning your phone call."

So he finally knew her last name. The revelation registered briefly before it was replaced by his excitement that she'd phoned. He found his voice.

"Hi. I'm glad you called back."

Garrett turned his chair, shifting so that his back was to Cliff. Thankfully Cliff was busy with his own phone call. "I'm sorry I didn't call you," Garrett apologized. "The case got crazy."

"I figured you were busy with work. I saw on the news that you guys made some arrests."

She was playing aloof. Garrett heard the control in her voice and suddenly was determined to change her attitude. "We arrested two men for the crimes. After that, I took a few days off to spend with my son. We went camping and my cell signal was sporadic." He paused. So much for making her loosen up. He doubted that explanation sounded plausible. "It sounds really lame, but it's the truth… How are you?"

"Fine," Olivia answered. Her fingers tightened on the black handset of her desk phone.

"I'm glad," Garrett said, not very satisfied with her vague answer. "This isn't going well, Olivia. I'm bombing here, aren't I?"

"It's fine," she said.

Fine. An annoying word if there ever was one. He took a deep breath. All she could do was say no to his offer, and if she did, he deserved it.

"I guess this is going to come across even worse. I don't have much time because I'm due in a meeting in five minutes, but before I let you go, are you free Saturday afternoon, say about one?"

"Why?" Olivia asked, her tone still flat. "I thought you only needed one date. You got that and more."

"I guess I deserved that," Garrett said. He shifted uncomfortably. "I would like to see you again, and not because of what happened that night. It's my division picnic, and I'd be honored if you'd join me. You can meet the people I work with, and my son will be with me."

"So, another date?" She sounded surprised.

Garrett reached for a pen and rolled it between his fingers. "Yes, if you'd be willing. You intrigue me

Olivia, and I'd really like to spend some time getting to know you better."

In her office, Olivia thought of Shane's cryptic words. If she accepted Garrett's offer, she'd have a legitimate excuse not to go to Sara's upcoming event. Olivia would also get to see Garrett again, and thus, she'd be able to decide if the passion she'd experienced had been just a one-time thing. Part of her had to know.

"Casual dress," Garrett said, as if sensing her weakening. "Like wear shorts," he added.

Olivia pondered for a moment. That night in her pool house had been special, and then he'd forgotten about her until now. Something else had been bothering her, as well. "You never told me why you only needed one date," she said.

There was a pause, and then Garrett said, "I lost a bet during a game of poker. The guys bet me to go on a date. Before you and I went out, I hadn't had a real date in at least three years—well, since I'd been divorced."

"I see." She remained skeptical. The picnic would be a public event, eliminating any temptation of a repeat of what had happened at her place. "This isn't just to parade me? Prove something? Because if slaking some lust was the only thing on your agenda that night—been there, done that. I'm not sure I'm up for another go-round."

"I deserved that, too," Garrett said with a wince. He twisted the phone cord. Olivia had just risen in his estimation. She wasn't like the others who had thrown themselves at him after the calendar debut. She was also direct, not the type to play games. In fact, he doubted she knew how to play them. While parts of her were contradictory, her innate integrity was crystal clear. She was a woman of principles. And he had botched things badly.

"I've been a heel, haven't I," Garrett said. "Please let me redeem myself. I really am interested in you, Olivia. I'd like to get to know you. We could just put in an appearance Saturday, then leave if you decide you aren't enjoying the picnic. Or we could simply skip it and go somewhere else. Matt wouldn't care."

The sincerity in his voice was obvious and Olivia wavered. She'd missed Garrett. She could imagine his scent on her couch. She could picture him sitting on the bar stool. She'd felt they had a connection. Maybe she should give him another chance. Attempting to be a bad girl had taught her one thing. She was in control of her future. Besides, this time his son would be along as a chaperon.

"Olivia?"

"I'm here. I'm debating," she admitted. "I'm trying to decide if this is wise."

"Leaning in my favor, I hope?"

"This time," she said, giving in to her desire to see him again. "I'll go."

She heard his sigh of relief. "The picnic is in Queeny Park. How about I come by your place at one and pick you up? Unless you'd rather meet me there?"

"One sounds good. You know the way. Would you like me to bring anything?"

"Nope. Everything's taken care of," Garrett said. He paused a moment. "Olivia?"

"Yes?" she asked.

"I'm horrible on the phone, but I'll try to call you this week if only to say hello. I'm extremely glad you're going. I'll see you Saturday."

"Saturday," she echoed as she hung up the phone.

She gave the chair a little spin and gazed out the window at the Gateway Arch, sighing and allowing herself one girlish giggle of delight. Then she turned, decided not to make anything more of the upcoming date, and focused. She knew she'd probably fail at that resolution as Saturday drew closer, but for now, with her meeting recommencing in ten minutes, she was determined to try. Garrett, and her thoughts of him, could wait.

WHEN GARRETT SWIVELED back around, Cliff was standing two feet away and staring at him.

"Did I just overhear you ask Olivia Jacobsen to the picnic?"

"As a matter of fact, you did. What of it?" Garrett said, immediately defensive and not certain he liked Cliff's disapproving attitude. "Wunderlich told me to bring a date, so I asked Olivia. We had a good time that night, I think she'll have fun and quite frankly, I'd like to see her again. Hell, Cliff, you should be thrilled for me. I just asked a woman out."

"You did what?" This outburst came from Pete, who was watching from his desk. "You asked a woman out, Garrett?"

Now everyone on the floor was staring at him. "Yes, I did. Is that so tough for everyone to believe?"

"Yeah," Pete said. "Moira won't. She'll have to meet your date herself to believe it. You're bringing her to the picnic?"

"If you all don't scare her off the moment we arrive, I am," Garrett said. Amused chuckles sounded from others seated nearby. "She's a nice girl."

"Ah, my Moira will keep everyone in line," Pete said with pride. "She's helping Trisha. Don't worry, Garrett. You'll be just fine. We'll all make sure, won't we, Cliff?"

"Yeah," Cliff said as he walked back to his desk.

Garrett frowned. What the heck was wrong with *him?* He glanced at the clock on his phone and jumped to his feet. He had a meeting to attend, and whatever had crawled up Cliff could wait. Garrett had a date, and nothing was going to spoil that.

Chapter Eight

The day of the picnic dawned clear and sunny. Anyone living in St. Louis knew that those two words usually meant hot and sticky, but this August day was surprisingly low in humidity, making it perfect for an outdoor event.

Garrett drove into Olivia's driveway exactly at one and, as she'd been pacing for the past fifteen minutes, she stepped out of the side door the moment he arrived and closed the door quickly behind her. The last thing Olivia desired was for Sara to swoop down. Under the guise of having a date—with the same man as previously—Olivia had wormed out of Sara's dinner party, but that didn't mean that Olivia was off the hook with Sara or ready to let Sara meet him.

In fact, if Garrett met her parents, the owners of the main house, Olivia knew she'd have some explaining to do, including how she wasn't really a counter girl. She wasn't ready to explain anything yet. Besides, if this date fizzled faster than day-old soda pop, it would not be necessary to expose her half truths. If the relationship continued, hopefully they would have a stronger foundation for her to reveal the truth.

As a PR person, Olivia knew that timing was everything. She'd seen too many people make mistakes by rushing into things or revealing too much too soon. She'd know when the best time was to tell Garrett the truth; she was sure of it. Everything would work out just fine at its own pace. They'd already gotten past his lack of phone contact. That was something.

As she approached Garrett's car, he opened the door and got near. He wore a navy polo shirt, khaki shorts and his tennis shoes. "Hi," she said, suddenly nervous.

"Hi right back," Garrett said, his gaze raking over her. "You are a sight for sore eyes."

"Thanks," she said. Awkwardness had her pressing her hands over an imaginary wrinkle in her tan shorts. Because she was going to a picnic, she'd chosen to wear a baby-blue ribbed T-shirt. She'd cuffed her white socks and stuffed her feet into white leather Keds tennis shoes. She'd gone for casual. She planned to make the perfect impression, if there really was such a thing.

Garrett came around and opened Olivia's door. His arm brushed hers, making her skin tingle. Leaning into the car, he introduced his son.

"Olivia, I'd like you to meet Matt. Matt, this is Olivia. She's going to the picnic with us."

"Hi, Olivia," Matt said.

"Hi," Olivia said as Garrett stepped aside. She slid

onto the seat and turned around. Matt Krause was a cute blond with intense blue eyes. He wore red shorts, a white T-shirt emblazoned with a fire truck and a baseball cap. "Are you excited to go to the picnic?" Olivia said.

"Yes," he said with a solemn nod.

"We haven't told him about the *P-O-O-L*," Garrett said, spelling the word as he got into the car. "We won't be doing any *S-W-I-M-M-I-N-G*, although some of the teens will."

"So this is an all-day event?" Olivia asked.

"Pretty much. It starts at one and people come and go all day. The diehards stay the entire time until the park closes."

"I'm going to go on a pony ride," Matt announced. "And bounce."

"There will be pony rides, some big inflatable bounce toys, and hayrides," Garrett explained as he started the car and drove west on Ladue Road. "The division goes all out for this. We have all sorts of adult activities—fishing, softball, sand volleyball—and we have games and races for the kids. It's fun."

Olivia nodded. It sounded, well, just as Garrett had said. Fun. Simple pleasures, the kind that her moneyed crowd thought beneath them. Soon Garrett was on Mason Road and pulling into the entrance to Queeny Park.

"There's never anyone parked over on this side," he said, as he pulled into a spot. After unhooking Matt, Garrett unloaded the trunk. He hoisted three bags of folding chairs onto his shoulder, then grabbed the handle of the cooler and yanked. The cooler made a grinding sound as the wheels bounced over the asphalt path. Matt ran alongside.

"I see our group over there," Garrett said, and he led the way to a group of tables underneath a large canopy. The area had one permanent picnic shelter, several large temporary canopies and two barbecue pits that sizzled with hamburgers, hotdogs and bratwursts. All around, people played horseshoes or Frisbee, or simply socialized. This type of event was foreign to Olivia. Her crowd held tent parties that were formal, catered affairs, with everyone dressed in corporate casual. Drinks weren't in aluminum cans or plastic cups but in glass champagne flutes. Here at Garrett's picnic, toss-away paper plates and plastic silverware were the norm, not china and sterling that some caterer would clean.

"Garrett, there you are." A fifty-something woman waved at him.

"Hi, Moira," Garrett said. He dragged the cooler over and set it next to a picnic table, then gave the petite woman a hug. "How are you?"

"Great. Pete's on barbecue duty, so I don't know if I'd eat anything if I were you. Ah, Matt. You've grown so much since last year!"

"I'm in junior kindergarten," Matt said with a big grin.

"Matt, you remember Mrs—"

"Miss Moira," she said, dimples widening. "Or

Miss M, if that's easier. That's simpler for Adam. My grandson is your age and he's over there digging in the sand. See?"

Matt's eyes followed the point of her finger to where a group of boys were digging in the sand volleyball court. A pile of tennis shoes lay nearby. "Dad? Can I?"

"You may go play with them," Garrett said, correcting Matt's grammar. "Just take off your shoes first."

"Yes, Dad." Matt whooped and ran over to the court. The children welcomed him immediately.

"Their shoes will be overflowing with sand whether they take them off or not. That's a given at these things," Moira said. Her gaze fell on Olivia. She coughed. "Garrett?" But Garrett was watching Matt join the boys, his protective stance never changing as his son settled into the game. Moira rolled her eyes. "Men," she said to Olivia. "Hi, I'm Moira. Pete Shepard's wife. He works with Garrett and they occasionally play poker together on Friday nights at my house."

"Occasionally?" Garrett said, his attention returning.

"Usually," Moira corrected. "You men could use some culture. Like the theater or something."

"I go to the movie theater," Garrett offered with a grin. "We play less poker than you play bunko."

"Don't be difficult," Moira said with a shake of her finger. "You know exactly what I meant."

"I'm Olivia," Olivia said, and she extended her hand. Moira laughed as she shook it, her handshake light.

"Such formality. Garrett, start loosening this girl up a little. Get her a beer or something."

"Actually, soda's fine," Olivia said. She really didn't like beer and her better judgment told her not to drink anything alcoholic. She'd already seduced the man sober; keeping a level head was in order tonight.

"No beer?" Moira arched an eyebrow. "Tell me, where'd you go to high school?"

"J.B." Olivia admitted.

"That explains everything," Moira said with a sage nod. "Well, if anyone can loosen you up, Garrett can. He worked wonders with Cliff. You'd never tell that Cliff came from riches, compared to the rest of us South Siders. He's older than Garrett by a few years. His family forced him to do a stint in their business before they gave up and let him join the police force."

"Do I hear my name being taken in vain?"

"Ah, Cliff," Moira said, enveloping him in a bear hug. "Speak of the devil. I wondered if you were coming."

"I wouldn't have missed this for the world." Cliff turned. "Garrett."

"Hey, Cliff. Olivia, this is Cliff, the man who, unfortunately, has the honor of being my best friend."

"Yeah, what can I say?" Cliff said with a wide grin. "I was desperate on pick-a-friend day."

"It's nice to meet you," Olivia said, this time keeping her hand next to her side as Cliff didn't seem too inclined to shake it.

She took a moment to study Cliff. He seemed

familiar, but Olivia couldn't place him. Built like a linebacker, he was probably close to forty. He stood taller than Garrett, and was a bit broader in the chest, as well. He wore a dark blue T-shirt and denim shorts, his feet stuck in low socks and cross-trainers.

"It's nice to meet you," Cliff said politely, his expression neutral. His attention moved immediately back to Garrett. "Is Matt here?"

"He's over there," Garrett said, gesturing toward the volleyball pit. Garrett winced. Using a yellow plastic shovel, Matt was filling a bucket. Everyone was shrieking, an indication that they were all having a great time as they dumped the buckets out. Garrett groaned. "He *is* going to be full of grit and grime."

"Of course he is," Moira said with a glance heavenward. "Didn't you hear me earlier? Well, there's no sense in cleaning your son now. Some of the teen girls have agreed to take them over to the playground about three. They'll come back even dirtier after that. Just give him a thorough scrub in the bath tonight when you get home."

"That sounds like a plan," Garrett said. He reached down, rummaged in the cooler and took out a cola for Olivia and domestic beers for him and for Cliff. He lobbed a can over to Cliff, who easily caught it. "Here you are," he said to Olivia, handing her a cold soda.

"Thanks," she said, her fingers zinging as his touched hers briefly.

"So Olivia, what do you do?" Cliff asked.

"I'm in communications," she said. Something about Cliff's tone bothered her.

"Olivia and I met when she was working behind the counter of the *Mound City Monitor*," Garrett explained.

Olivia observed the expression in Garrett's eyes, an obvious warning directed at Cliff.

Moira seemed oblivious to the undercurrent between the men, or perhaps she was just used to the way they interacted. "That's sweet," Moira said. "Well, welcome to the group, Olivia. Even though they're cops, they're actually all teddy bears, so don't let any of them treat you otherwise."

"A teddy bear? Yeah, like that's it," Cliff said. He didn't appear amused. "On that note, I'm going to see how the food's coming."

"I think I'll join you," Garrett said. "To make sure Pete hasn't ruined the steaks." He followed Cliff toward the barbecue pit and caught up with him after a few paces. "What's your problem?" Garrett asked, his voice low.

"Nothing," Cliff said, but the tension in his shoulders indicated differently.

"Yeah, wrong," Garrett said. "I'm not sure why you've got such a burr about Olivia, but today lay off her."

Without breaking his stride, Cliff turned and arched an eyebrow. "Did you hear what Moira asked? Your sweetheart went to J. B. High School. I went to J.B. Did you ever consider that I might think you set this all up?"

"I had no idea who Olivia was when I met her,"

Garrett said. He tried to read Cliff's expression, but could see only anger.

"Well, if that's the truth, then you have no idea who she is now, do you? For a detective, you're pretty lousy. My suggestion is that you should probably find out more about Olivia Jacobsen before you fall into her clutches."

"Why don't you just put on the table what you're trying to say?"

But they'd reached the guys surrounding the barbecue pit, and that meant any chance of a private conversation had evaporated. Cliff ignored Garrett's scowl and quickly assimilated himself into the group of men. Garrett resolved to get to the bottom of this mystery later. It wasn't as if he didn't know where Cliff worked.

"So is that her?" Pete asked, peering through the mirrored sunglasses that dominated his face.

Moira really should tell her hubby that those went of fashion two decades ago. "That's Olivia," Garrett said. He took a long sip of his beer as Pete used some tongs to roll the bratwursts over.

"She's pretty," Pete said.

"I kind of think so," Garrett agreed as he gazed over at where Olivia sat with Moira. Pale blue was a color that suited her, and the ribbed T-shirt revealed her curves—curves his body remembered well… He checked those thoughts. Now was not the time or place.

"You could do worse," Pete remarked.

Garrett nodded. The difference between Olivia and Brenda was even more obvious now that Moira had seated Olivia at a table of wives. As Olivia laughed at something someone said, he could see that they'd already accepted her. No one had ever accepted Brenda. She'd always been too snobbish, had considered herself too above everyone else in social status.

Olivia was natural. Unpretentious. Oh, there was a refinement to her that was a credit to her upbringing, and Garrett now knew her upbringing was one of the secrets she was keeping from him. Too many paradoxes still swirled around her, including where she went to high school. She'd gone to J.B., an exclusive prep school. But unlike Cliff, who'd made his distrust clear, Garrett wasn't throwing up red flags. He'd felt nothing other than an inkling telling him to beware, which he'd already dismissed as insignificant.

Right now, Garrett simply wanted to enjoy the day and his time with this woman. Besides, he wasn't planning to fall in love. From this point on, he would take things slow, as slow as one could after one had made love on the first date. For a moment Garrett entertained the thought that maybe Olivia would be willing to have a relationship with no strings. Then he dismissed the idea.

Her personality wasn't conducive to that, and in reality, neither was his. No, he could tell Olivia threw herself into everything, just as she was now devoting herself to Matt and using a wet wipe to clean his ice-cream-covered face. From the way she handled Matt,

Garrett could see Olivia liked children and wasn't just tolerating his son in order to get closer to Garrett.

Maybe, just maybe, he had found someone special this time.

"Hey, Garrett, can you come help us get the bounce thing set up?" someone called.

"Sure," Garrett said. Olivia was with Moira, which meant she was in capable hands.

THE MOMENT GARRETT went off to help inflate the bounce pit, Cliff waited for all of two seconds before he made his way back to the picnic table. It was time to expose his hand, but not necessarily with Garrett around. One thing Cliff had learned from being part of St. Louis upper-crust society: sometimes you just had to do the dirty work yourself. And that meant dealing with Olivia. Cliff had always had an issue with liars, and Olivia was pulling a huge con. She could not simply continue to delude his best friend.

"Olivia," Cliff said as he slid onto the bench across from her. She'd been left alone for a moment, making his timing perfect. "Olivia Jacobsen—that is your name?"

She smiled at him tentatively. Cliff grimaced just once. He hated being an ass, but he had to protect Garrett. Good old Garrett, who despite his best intentions couldn't fend off someone like Olivia. The man had simply ignored where Olivia had gone to high school, proving that he was already in way too deep.

"Cliff Jones. You and I met once, ages ago. You know my cousin Austin."

"Oh, yes." Her face clouded as she tried to figure out where he was going with this.

"You were engaged to him," Cliff said. He shifted into interrogation mode and leaned forward. "Olivia, do me a favor. Tell me, what were doing behind the desk at the *Monitor?*"

"Helping out a friend," Olivia said.

Cliff gave her credit for having a backbone as she refused to back out of the conversation.

"My friend Chrissy needed to leave momentarily."

Cliff's expression didn't change. "And you still work for Jacobsen Enterprises?"

"Yes," Olivia said. She put both her hands in her lap, her shoulders rigid.

"Garrett doesn't know that. What kind of a stunt are you pulling?"

"I'm not." She met his gaze defiantly. "The circumstances of our meeting are none of your business and I'll clear everything up when the time is right. If this date fizzled, there would be no point."

"Olivia, Garrett Krause is the nicest guy I know. The last thing he needs is to discover you're lying. He's not in our social class. He doesn't play by our rules."

Fury crossed her face. "I'm not…"

"Do you know why he asked you out? He lost a bet. He had to go on a date. We sent him to place a personal ad, and instead he went out with you."

She didn't blink, and he could tell she was ticked. "And your point is?"

Cliff had to give her credit. When you raised

Olivia's ire, the gloves did come off. "My point is that all Garrett had to do was save face with the guys. That's done. I don't want to see him hurt again. He's already had one society wife. Been there, done that. He swore he'd never do it again. So you can see why this charade concerns me. He's dating you without realizing who you really are."

Olivia held herself straight. She really had made a disaster of things, hadn't she? She'd wanted to be bad—and in doing so she'd created a terrible mess.

"Garrett already told me he only needed one date," she said flatly. She pressed down her shoulders as she rallied. "And we had that date at Melanie's. When he called me about today, he told me about the bet. As for me, I'm not up to anything except getting to know someone."

"Under false pretenses," Cliff said. He rose. "Olivia, either you tell Garrett who you are, or I do. I'm not going to stand by and watch him develop feelings for someone who has lied to him."

She bristled at that. "You don't even know me."

"Maybe not," Cliff said. "But I know Garrett. He's just now trying to get back on the scene after an ugly divorce. She was like you, rich and spoiled. She lied. She betrayed him. Garrett values integrity—and she shredded her vows. You can't keep deluding him. You'll devastate him. And I don't want to see him set him back another three years."

She felt her expression frozen in place. "I think you are very kind for caring so much, but if you are truly

his friend, you should let Garrett make his own decisions."

Cliff stood there for a moment. "Have you seen the
calendar?"

She nodded. Honesty was fine here. "I saw it that
day at the *Monitor*. Chrissy had it."

He shifted his weight. "Women threw themselves
at him after that hit the stores. He's quite jaded about
bold and brassy women."

Olivia thought of her blatant proposition.

"So tell me," Cliff said, "why are you really with
him?"

Angered and unsettled by the whole vein of the
conversation, she snapped, "Sex."

Cliff had the gall to snort. "Oh, please. Spare me."
And with that, he turned on his heel and walked off.

Olivia sat there for a moment. She'd shot her mouth
off to Sara the morning after and now she'd shot off a
glib reply to Cliff. She wasn't sure she liked the person
she was fast becoming—Olivia Jacobsen, liar.

"You can certainly tell we're at a police function,"
Moira said as she moved to stand beside Olivia. Both
Moira and Olivia watched Cliff walk away. "Do you
know how you can always tell a cop?"

"No," Olivia said. Her gaze sought out Garrett. He
was still helping to inflate the bounce pit.

"You can tell from their walk. Their arms are always
a little out from their sides. That comes from not
wanting to chafe against the gun belt. They carry themselves differently, a statement of their dominance.

Criminals say they can spot a cop a mile away just from his walk."

"I never noticed anything like that with Garrett," she said.

"Nah," Moira said. "He was promoted off the beat pretty quickly and has been plainclothes ever since. He's one of the best detectives the department has. Garrett's a thinker. He analyzes everything from all angles before making a move."

Except with her, Olivia thought. With her, Garrett had jumped in feet first. He'd simply accepted a bunch of half truths and made some outright assumptions. How would he react when he learned the truth? Her father had always insisted that honesty was the best policy—but was it already too late for that?

Garrett caught her gaze and waved. Her heart gave a little jump.

"He's a great guy," Moira said before walking away. "One of the best. I can already tell you're going to be very good for him."

Now alone, Olivia bit her lip, remorse consuming her. She was trapped between the proverbial rock and hard place. Fate seemed to have placed Garrett in her life for a reason. At this moment, though, Olivia felt simply nothing but guilt. She'd led Garrett on. She'd slept with him. And here she was, his date at his division picnic. By bringing her, he'd brought her into his world, a world so very different from her own. She was an interloper. She didn't belong.

Cliff's words were having their desired effect. Olivia was now full of doubts. Did she really think she could fit in a world like this after all her deceptions?

Maybe she should make this the final date and return to her boring but safe life. The last thing she wanted was to hurt Garrett; that would be unforgivable. She watched as he helped the first group of kids enter the inflated bounce pit. One thing was clear: she already cared way too much.

"Olivia? The food is about ready. Can you help me set up the buffet?"

Olivia rose to her feet. "Sure. I'd be happy to."

She would let herself enjoy today. She'd give herself that much. Then perhaps it was be time for the prodigal daughter to return home.

Chapter Nine

"So are you having fun?" Garrett asked Olivia, about five-thirty. The past four hours had been busy ones. They'd eaten, and Olivia had kicked off her shoes and played a darn good game of sand volleyball. She hadn't been very good at washers, though, which was a middle-class St. Louis game similar to horseshoes. The idea was to toss steel washers, those half-dollar-size metal rings used in construction, into a coffee can. The can was placed in the middle of a two-by-two-foot box, and Olivia had overshot the target.

What had impressed Garrett was how easily she'd taken defeat and how she'd laughed at her ineptness at the game. Brenda had been livid and had refused to play ever again.

"We should have bet," he'd teased Olivia earlier.

"Then I'd owe you something."

"Exactly," Garrett had replied with a grin designed to wiggle her toes. He hoped it had.

In a public place, getting to know her had been difficult—the one downfall of inviting her to the picnic. People had surrounded them at all times and someone was always coming up to say hello. Olivia had tolerated the attention well, and Garrett had been pleased with how perfectly she'd fit in. Moira had even come up to Garrett privately and said, "I like this one. She's a keeper."

Now Garrett finally had Olivia alone, or as alone as one could be on the path that led toward the playground, where Matt still played under the watchful eyes of a group of teenage girls.

Olivia seemed distracted.

"So you haven't been overwhelmed?" he asked.

"A little, but I've had a wonderful time," Olivia said. He fell in step beside her. "Everyone you work with is so nice. Moira especially."

"We're like a family," Garrett said. "Moira's everyone's second mom."

"I work for a family-owned firm, but it's nothing like this," Olivia said. Her Keds made a thumping sound on the asphalt path. "You're extremely lucky. I don't consider the people in my department my close friends. Acquaintances yes, but not friends. People to gossip with, but not to hang out with."

"I guess we are different. We are close. I'd trust all these guys with my life. Cliff and I have known each other since the academy. He was my best man." Garrett contemplated that for a moment. He'd never really thought about his work in this context. "Maybe the nature of the job makes us like a family. The shifts we work and the dangers we can face mean that we have to depend on one another. I know I can trust every guy in there." He paused. "I couldn't say the same about my ex-wife. She was out jockeying for someone new before we'd even filed divorce papers."

Which was why Cliff had warned Olivia off. She understood Cliff's actions perfectly, though understanding didn't make her current situation easier. "You're very lucky to have such a great support system," she said.

"I am," Garrett agreed. "The people I work with are the best. They liked you, you know. Moira told me so."

Olivia was saved from commenting, for she and Garrett had reached the playground. Matt immediately spotted his dad.

"Hey, Dad! Watch me go down the slide," he shouted.

"Show me," Garrett said.

Matt displayed his sliding skills, and Olivia found a spot on a bench to sit as Garrett joined his son on the playground.

Observing Garrett's interaction with his son was an enlightening experience. The man was a hands-on type of father. He pushed Matt on the swings, climbed through some tunnels and once even went down the slide with him. Garrett didn't worry about what any onlookers might be thinking—his concentration was solely on his son and for his son's happiness. Olivia swallowed. She couldn't remember her father being around like that.

"Hey, Olivia!" Matt yelled. "Watch me! This one's for you!"

"I'm watching!" She clapped after Matt slid down stomach first. When he was back on his feet, Matt laughed and bowed.

As she continued to observe Matt play, Olivia had a sudden insight. She'd been about Matt's age when Sara came into her life. As Matt had done just a moment ago with Garrett, had Olivia sought out Sara's approval?

Being so young, Olivia had accepted Sara's presence in the family without question. But she had grown up wishing for Sara's approval and had tried to be perfect—up until a few weeks ago when, at the late age of thirty, she'd rebelled. Until then, her good behavior had been a way of seeking acceptance.

A memory flowed into Olivia's consciousness. Blake had come home from a mission trip; even with a nanny, Sara had had a grueling day. Shane had come along pretty quickly after her father's new marriage, and Bethany and Claire often had argued. Two step siblings fighting and a new baby had consumed a lot of Sara's time. Olivia's father had ruffled her hair that day. "Sara says you were the only good one. I'm glad I can count on you. You're Daddy's girl."

And Olivia had strived from that moment on to be perfect. Grandpa Joe was correct. She'd lived her life trying to please everyone but herself.

"Ready?" Garrett asked as he and Matt approached.

"Yes." She rose for the walk back to the picnic area.

"I hope you weren't too bored."

"No." Sitting there had been eye opening.

"He likes you," Garrett said, as Matt ran ahead down the path. "I think he has great taste."

Two of Garrett's co-workers approached from behind, ending the private moment as they joined Olivia and Garrett.

The evening drew to a close a little later, and Matt climbed up into her arms, hugged her and within an instant was fast asleep.

"You have kids?" Moira asked as she brought Olivia a napkin to put under Matt's open mouth.

"Nieces and nephews," Olivia said, shifting Matt slightly.

"Well, you're a natural, honey," Moira said. "You remind me of my daughter Katherine."

Moira moved off to clean up. It was almost seven o'clock, and many people had already cleared out. Only the diehards remained. While some still played games, most had settled around picnic tables for food and conversation. Cliff was long gone; Olivia hadn't seen him since early afternoon.

"We should probably get Matt home," Garrett said as he returned from deflating the bounce pit. "He's usually in bed by eight, so this is late for him."

"He's worn out," Olivia noticed.

"I'll go put the stuff in the car and then come back and carry him," Garrett said. He reached for the cooler handle.

"It's fine. I've got him." Olivia rose to her feet.

"Are you sure?"

"Positive," she replied. Matt was heavy, but she carried him easily. She winced only once as he bumped against her hip. She now understood why nature put lots of weight on women's hips after childbirth.

"He's going to tire you. Let me carry him."

"No," Olivia insisted. She'd discovered there was something special about having a child sleeping on your shoulder. "I've got him. I'm actually enjoying this. It's, well, practice."

The cooler wheels ground over the path. "So you want kids?"

The loaded question didn't scare Olivia. "Oh, definitely. I grew up in a large family. My mother died when I was young. My father had me, my twin, Nick, and my sister, Claire. Then he remarried, to a woman who had a daughter my age, and together they had my brother Shane. He's five years younger. How about you?"

"Just me and my younger sister, Anna. She's married to some guy she met in college, and lives in Bloomington. They have two children."

"So you're an uncle."

"Yep." They'd reached the car. Garrett opened the driver's door and started the engine and the air-conditioner, leaving the door open so the built-up heat could escape. He then opened the back door and took Matt from Olivia's arms. He situated his son in the booster seat and strapped him in. Matt's head lolled to the left, but he never woke up. Garrett put the cooler in the trunk. "Thanks for being so great with Matt."

"You're welcome." The compliment was meaningful. Garrett trusted her with his son. "I like being an aunt. Aunt Livvy, the kids call me," she said. "My brother Shane started that nickname when he was little. He never could pronounce Olivia. The name's stuck."

"Livvy." Garrett shook his head as he closed the trunk. "I like Olivia better. It suits you."

"It means 'olive.' I'm not sure that's very exciting," Olivia said. "My dad's a minister. There aren't any relatives named Olivia in my family, so I always think of the olive branch, or even the Mount of Olives."

"Mount of Olives? That sounds familiar."

"Jesus told the disciples about the end of the age there. It's east of Jerusalem and higher than Mount Zion. Supposedly its summit commands a great view of the city and temple. I told you my dad's a minister. He can read Hebrew and Greek."

"So you're a P.K.," Garrett said. He leaned his hip against the car so he could study her.

"I'm a preacher's kid," Olivia acknowledged. A waft of air-conditioning drifted from the open car door.

"It can't be any worse than being a cop's kid," Garrett said. "I never ran afoul of the law when I was growing up or my dad would have had my hide."

"I grew up hearing exactly what being bad got you," Olivia admitted.

Now that the interior of the car was cooling off, Garrett closed both doors on the driver's side. He and Olivia stood outside the car. "So did you rebel?" he asked.

She couldn't tell him no. She arched an eyebrow, instead, and asked, "Did you?"

Garrett gave, a wide smile that caused Olivia to flush. "I think your restrictions were probably greater than mine. We rarely went to church except on holy days. So long as my actions were legal, I could do pretty much anything. My dad had a 'boys will be boys' attitude to a lot of things, as long as he considered them normal adolescent behavior. He worked on the North Side of St. Louis City, so he saw a lot of gritty street action."

"I admit, I was a good girl," Olivia said ruefully. "That Billy Joel song fit me to a *T*. It's difficult to be bad when you have the world praying for your redemption. My younger brother—now, he was a different story. Me, I'm the good one."

Garrett strode around the car and into Olivia's personal space. "I think you are *very* good."

Olivia's breath caught in her throat. "How so?"

"Oh, you're like good news. You make me smile. You seem too good to be true, but you aren't. You kiss me and that feels very good, and what we did the other night—that was exceedingly good."

"I see," Olivia said, her body already humming in anticipation.

"I see, too," Garrett said. He reached forward to trace her jawbone with his and forefinger. "I see a very beautiful woman in front of me who has been tempting me all day. I'm not used to being tempted."

"That doesn't sound very good," Olivia said.

"Oh, but it is," Garrett replied, his voice husky. "It means you've drawn something from inside me. I'm probably laying my cards on the table way too quickly, but I want to see you again. I want to get to know you better. If you are planning to let me down, then do it now."

"I just want you to kiss me," Olivia said. Where had those words come from?

But Olivia had no time to figure that out. Garrett's lips swooped down to capture hers. He kissed her solidly. Desire immediately flared, but had to be tamped down because they were standing in a parking lot.

"Now that was a good idea," he said as he finally let her go.

Olivia's lips still tingled.

"It was probably a good idea to stop before we got too carried away. I know I wanted to continue." He opened her door and seated her before going around to the driver's side. "Matt makes a good chaperon."

Olivia glanced into the back seat. Matt slept on, oblivious to the kiss his father had just given her. "He's a sweetheart," she said.

"One of the best things that ever happened to me," Garrett said. "He's my pride and joy."

"I can tell," Olivia said.

The return trip to Olivia's pool house seemed to take less time than getting to the park had, and they arrived long before Olivia wanted the conversation she and Garrett were having in the car to end. She'd seen lights up at the main house, meaning her parents' party was still in full swing.

"Maybe you can bring Matt over for a swim sometime," she offered, as Garrett put the car in park.

"He'd like that," Garrett said. "We'll plan for it. But next I want to do something that's just us. I'll call you, and this time it won't take two weeks."

"I'd understand if it did," Olivia said. "You're the type of guy who means what he says."

"I am, and I plan to see you again, Olivia. I'm serious about that. If that's okay with you."

"Sounds like a good idea." She parroted his earlier words about dating back to him so that the intense moment didn't seem so surreal.

"She mocks me," Garrett said teasingly, and leaned over to give Olivia a lingering kiss that sent shivers through her body.

The man could kiss, and if one of them didn't stop she'd be dragging him inside.

"God, I hate to let you out of the car," Garrett said huskily. He touched her cheek gently, and then with a groan of determination, he reached for his door handle. Within seconds he helped her get out. The moment she stepped out of the car, Garrett drew her into his arms for another long kiss. After concentrated effort, he managed to put her at least a foot away from him.

"I hate to go, but I've got to get Matt to bed. I'll talk to you later."

"You'd better," Olivia said. She stood rooted to the spot as Garrett got back in the car and drove away.

Once the Malibu was out of sight she didn't go inside immediately. Instead, she kicked off her shoes and socks and waded onto the first step of the pool. Cool water played between her toes, washing away any residual sand.

Aside from Cliff's troubling words, today had been a great day. She'd enjoyed meeting everyone.

She sat down on the pool edge and dangled her legs in the water. She kicked her feet idly as she studied the haven that Jacobsen money had created. Even though she'd been born to this lifestyle, it didn't fit her. Oh, having a cleaning lady and a pool certainly did. But the way she lived rang as false as a three-dollar bill.

She existed in an insulated world of wealth and privilege. She didn't budget and could shop without worrying about price tags. She resided where the grass was very green and tended by a horticultural service. But the people she'd met today had something Olivia didn't have. Bonds. Ties. Genuine concern for one another. They'd created a family that would put their lives on the line for one another.

Olivia had no doubt her family would do that. But her friends? Her work colleagues? Never. The division picnic had shown Olivia one thing: home truly was wherever you hung your heart.

Until today Olivia had never recognized that she was simply skimming the surface of life. She had stuff, not substance. She had connections, not relationships. She had chains, not ties.

She'd thought losing her virginity would make her into something new and exciting. But in reality, she didn't need to be bad, but to be better about what she did.

She'd been so focused on how dull everyone in her circle was that she'd forgotten to address her own flaws. She was the one who'd failed. She'd failed to be her own person, had failed to be faithful to herself.

Cliff's harsh words had shaken her earlier, and since then, they hadn't been far from her thoughts. With Garrett she'd wanted to step out of her world, even if it meant hiding who she was. She'd been living a lie.

There was one thing that being a bad girl had brought her—while her motivations had been terrible, she'd met Garrett. She'd wanted him, and she'd gotten him.

But the victory was hollow. She'd won him because she'd avoided the truth, something she'd been raised never to do. He thought her a preacher's kid, a counter girl who rented a pool house.

However cruel Cliff's stinging barbs, they had been correct. She had to tell Garrett that she wasn't all that she'd portrayed herself to be—and soon.

Fear gripped her as the bitter realization hit. In her quest for immediate self-fulfillment, she'd ruined her chances for long-term happiness. She'd only been after one night, and while it hadn't been how she'd planned it, oh, how had she gotten that one night of sexual fulfillment.

But now that she wanted more, now that she had figured out whom she wanted to be with, was it too late to salvage a real relationship?

Garrett Krause valued personal integrity above everything else. Honesty and trust—she'd exhibited neither thus far. He'd feel betrayed if she told him everything now, including how rich she was.

Cliff had said Garrett was just now getting back into the dating game. If her secrets were exposed, he'd be upset. Olivia had been raised not to hurt people. And she'd tried, but being human, she'd failed. Perhaps it would be best to end things now, before everyone's emotions became tangled. Even though tonight had been perfect, perhaps she should put a lid on the relationship before it went any further.

If she kept seeing Garrett, she would only end up hurting him. She refused to let that happen. No, ending it now was the best choice. Then she wouldn't betray him with the truth. If, God forbid, her extensive deceptions were revealed, the comparison would be complete.

She'd be exactly like his ex-wife.

WHEN HE LIVED HERE years ago, this little corner of the world had been his favorite. A cool breeze flitted through the secluded arbor just off the stone path that led from the main house to the pool house. No one spent much time here anymore, except the gardener.

A series of trellises formed a roof for the five-by-five-foot space. From above, all one saw was a blanket of roses, creating a hideaway that, if one pushed the vines aside, provided an excellent view of the pool house and its private drive. It was the only spot on the estate that really had a clear view. Joe chuckled. Obviously Sara had no idea that this spot was here, or she would have installed a video camera to monitor Shane's antics. Or Olivia's. Joe had just been witness to a pretty passionate kiss.

Joe was not one to forget a face, and he'd recognized the man Olivia had been with as one who'd been featured in that charity calendar.

Since his granddaughter Claire had been one of the main organizers of the calendar, Joe had bought one himself in a show of support. He'd given it to his wife, Henrietta, for a joke. After over fifty years of marriage, one could do those things. The joke had been on him, as she'd immediately hung the calendar up in an out-of-the-way corner of the pantry. This month the pages revealed Mr. August, the man who had, moments ago, been kissing Olivia.

Joe hummed to himself, the same off-key musical number that always entered his head whenever he finally had all the puzzle pieces. He'd promised his wife that he wouldn't meddle—and he wouldn't break that promise. Especially since he knew exactly where to find the information he needed, and how to have someone else use it for him.

Chapter Ten

"Olivia, you have a call on line one. Garrett Krause. He says it's urgent and to please pick up."

The moment her secretary's voice resounded through the speaker at a little after noon, Olivia stared at her office phone as if the black plastic would somehow tell her what to do. She'd been dreading his call all week.

She'd managed to avoid talking to him since Sunday, but it hadn't been easy. She'd let all his calls go to her cell-phone voice mail. However, she'd made the mistake of listening to the messages, and just hearing his friendly voice had made her want to cry with futility. She had felt so guilty about ignoring him that she'd finally sent one text message: "Been busy. Will try to call soon."

She'd known when she sent the message that she wouldn't phone. Like that guy at the end of a date who says he'll call, then doesn't, it was coward's way to say goodbye. Without contact, everything would simply fizzle without anyone having to say the words. He wouldn't call, neither would she, and they'd both move on. She'd go back to her steady but boring life. Already Sara had plans to drop a few more eligible men into Olivia's lap.

This was Olivia's "normal." It was a lifestyle she was, if nothing else, comfortable in. Garrett Krause made her uncomfortable. He made her question her world, yearn to step outside it. He'd gotten to her. With him she wanted to feel every emotion, abandon herself to him and for a while simply be madly in love.

The picnic had shown her that was impossible. She couldn't change who she was any more than a leopard could change its spots. Besides, as she'd convinced herself just last night, she'd been smart in breaking any chance of a relationship off early. She was probably moving to New York City to take that position at O'Brien Publications, especially since her grandfather had pretty much indicated the job was Olivia's if she sat for the interview. How could she start a love affair with Garrett when she knew she wouldn't be around? How could she knowingly break her heart, and worse, his?

"Olivia?" Her secretary sounded frantic. "Are you there? He's on hold."

The flashing red light next to line one kept blinking, and Olivia bit her lip. She'd worn a blue power suit today, but that didn't necessarily give her any extra confidence. She didn't want to pick up the phone, didn't want to have to tell him she couldn't see him again. Why couldn't he have just disappeared, like the others? Why did she have to care for him?

The fact that she did care had come as another blow this week. Olivia had realized she'd fallen in love, and to a man she'd only hurt if he hung around her long enough. She'd ignored his phone messages, which each time had been akin to sending her heart through a paper shredding.

And now he'd again contacted her, this time declaring it was urgent.

What if something truly was wrong? Could she live with herself if she ignored him?

"I've got it," Olivia said. She picked up the receiver and pressed the button for line one. She remained standing, which gave her a feeling of control as she pushed her chair out of the way, took a deep breath and said, "This is Olivia Jacobsen."

"OLIVIA." When Garrett heard her voice, raw relief washed over him. He'd been so afraid she wouldn't pick up. He knew she'd been avoiding him, but he had no choice and no time to ask her why. She was his last hope.

"Garrett?"

He gripped the phone tighter and plunged ahead. "Thank God I finally caught you. I need a huge favor. Are you able to baby-sit Matt tonight?"

"What?"

He'd shocked her, but that didn't matter so long as she said yes. "Matt, my son. He knows you, and I've already tried everyone else. There's no one who can help me."

"Garrett, what is going on?" Olivia asked.

He was seated at his desk, and had to admit he was nervous. She hadn't called him back all week, and the one measly text-message she'd sent him was pretty clear. He hadn't planned to ask her to babysit, and this wasn't a ploy to see her again. He meant what he'd said; she was his last hope aside from using an impersonal babysitting service. He hated leaving Matt with some stranger, even if the person was licensed and bonded.

"I've been assigned to do a stakeout tonight starting at four this afternoon. I wasn't supposed to be working, but Gary's wife went into labor early. Unfortunately stakeouts aren't things that can be rescheduled, so the captain assigned me. Problem is, my mother is at the lake, Pete's on duty elsewhere, Moira is at her sister's, and my ex-wife and her family went to the Hamptons. That means I've got Matt. His day care closes at six, and I can't be there." Garrett took a quick breath. "If you could watch him for me, I'd be eternally grateful."

Atonement, Olivia thought as he finished. She could help him and this would be her penance for having to leave him. "I'm happy to help," she said.

As SHE WAITED for his response, her feet suddenly hurt. Whoever said designer shoes were comfy had been untruthful. "Just tell me where to go. My schedule's pretty flexible today."

She heard his audible sigh, indicating she'd alleviated some of his stress. "Just be at the Clayton Child Center by six tonight. I'll call them and tell them you're coming. You'll have to show your ID and sign him out."

"I did that once for my niece and nephew at their center. It'll be fine. I can handle babysitting," Olivia said. She grabbed a mechanical pencil. The metal was cool between her fingers. "Should I take him to my house?"

"Would you mind bringing him to mine?" Garrett asked. "He goes to sleep around eight and it'll be so much better to put him in his own bed. In about five minutes, I'm going to go home and try to catch a brief nap. I can leave a key under the mat."

"That's not very safe," Olivia observed.

Garrett laughed. "I know—I'm a cop. But for tonight, it'll work. I am in a safe area, and Gwen lives downstairs and she'll be home. She's eighty and not able care for Matt, but she's a great watchdog. I'll also leave all emergency numbers by the home phone. Once I'm on stakeout, you won't be able to reach me."

"I'll need directions."

"Got a piece of paper?"

"Yes," Olivia said. She wrote down directions to the child-care center and to Garrett's house. He actually lived directly across the street from Tower Grove Park.

"My house fronts Kingshighway," he told her. "Make a right on Magnolia, and it's on the corner. You'll see a huge wooden privacy fence. Magnolia has an island running down it, so go to the first U-turn, double back and park on the street. You'll find that easier than entering the alley and parking back by the garage. Go through the gate in the fence and I'll have Gwen leave the back door open. Upstairs, the key will be under the mat."

"Sounds easy enough," Olivia said.

"It will be, I promise," Garrett replied. "I can't thank you enough for doing this. If all goes well, we should be done by midnight."

"That's fine. I'll see you then." Olivia hung up the phone and gazed down at her desk. None of the reports she had to write held any appeal. She glanced down at her power suit. She should probably go home and change clothes before she got Matt. Grabbing her leather desk chair and pulling it toward the desk, she sat with a *thump*. Maybe she and Matt could do McDonald's for dinner. That would kill some time, and kids loved the play area. She'd miss her five-mile Friday-night run, but under the circumstances, she didn't mind.

She'd be seeing Garrett again—one last time, before she'd have to tell him that she couldn't see him again...and she wasn't looking forward to that.

Penance. She returned to her thought. Doing without Garrett Krause was her penance.

"OLIVIA!" Matt broke into a run the moment he saw her. He tossed himself into her arms and gave her a huge hug.

Was this warm-and-fuzzy sensation what her sister

Bethany experienced when she picked up her children? That feeling of being loved and wanted?

"You're here!" he exclaimed.

"Of course I am," Olivia said. She'd gone home to change clothes first, and now wore a short-sleeved sweater and camp shorts. She returned his hug. "I thought we'd go out for dinner."

"McDonald's," Matt said, grabbing her hand.

"Is there any other place?" Olivia asked. "I figured you'd like to play a bit."

"I do," Matt said. "I have a swing set in my backyard at Dad's house, but it's no fun all by myself."

"I can understand that," Olivia said. Since she'd already signed Matt out, they walked out to the parking lot.

Matt whistled. "Wow! Nice car!"

"Thanks," Olivia said. She did like her Saab, her age-defying gift to herself last year when she turned thirty.

"Can we put the top down?"

"Sure." It was hot and sticky outside and using the air conditioner would be more efficient, but why not let Matt have some fun? After all, she wouldn't be seeing him again.

That thought still tormented her, even hours later, as Olivia tucked Matt into bed around eight. The boy had been an absolute angel. They'd gotten to his house around seven-fifteen. Gwen had popped her head out of her place to get a glimpse of Olivia, had said hello to Matt and made conversation for a few seconds. Then Olivia and Matt had come upstairs.

Matt had his routine down pat. He'd watched half a television show, taken a bath, brushed his teeth and climbed into bed with a heap of books.

Olivia had read him several, including *Clifford the Big Red Dog* and *Mama Cat Has Three Kittens*. Then she'd said good-night, turned on his baseball night-light, switched off the overhead light and returned to the living room.

Garrett's brick two-family building was large. He lived upstairs and Gwen rented the first floor. Olivia assumed they both shared the basement—when she and Matt had walked in the back door, they'd passed the stairs leading to a lower level.

Unlike modern houses that didn't have many windows, Garrett had a bank of windows on the front wall, overlooking Tower Grove Park. He had two other large picture windows in the side wall, overlooking Magnolia Avenue: one in the living area, one in the dining area.

An arched beam separated the living and dining areas. The flat's only bathroom was on the other side of the dining-room wall, and after that came the kitchen.

The flat had two bedrooms, and Garrett had given Matt the master. Matt's bedroom was decorated in a baseball theme that included a St. Louis Cardinals comforter on his bed and autographed Cardinal posters on the walls.

Garrett had taken the second, smaller bedroom. In reality, if one counted the enclosed sunporch just off the bedroom, his tan-and-green bedroom was made up of two rooms. It contained a queen-size bed and a dresser.

She didn't linger in his room; viewing his bed gave her too many wicked thoughts. Instead she went back to the living room. Unlike many older city flats, this one had central air-conditioning, an expensive upgrade that must have been added after the place was built. Olivia had noticed that most places nearby had window units.

The living room didn't contain much furniture: a twenty-seven-inch television, a couch, a love seat and a coffee table. The dining room table wasn't too fancy, either. Garrett's apartment was furnished in bachelor-pad basic.

She grimaced. His ex-wife had probably taken the good stuff. A police officer didn't make big bucks, and who knew how much Garrett paid for child support. Not that his finances were Olivia's business, but she still found herself a bit angry.

However, Garrett Krause was not a man who needed rescuing. If anything, the person requiring saving was Olivia herself. This was how the other half lived, and she'd been oblivious. Thoughts of her life of wealth and privilege irked her anew.

How could she expect to have a relationship with Garrett? He was a man who'd carved out a niche in his own world. He wouldn't move back into a world like his ex-wife's.

But the biggest difference between Olivia and him was their choice of occupations. What Garrett did truly mattered. He worked to keep the bad guys off the streets, like tonight. Olivia pushed paper that made everyone more money.

Yet as she sat there on the middle-class couch that probably came from a discount furniture store, she realized that his flat was more of a home than where she lived. Pictures of Matt dominated every surface. Garrett himself was in some of them, and he was usually smiling and laughing. The man was gorgeous and happy. And he was the man she loved.

But while she knew she love him easily, she'd learned that she wasn't good at relationships. Despite her newfound understanding of herself, there was no way she was going to risk hurting Garrett Krause. He was a good man, much too good for her.

She flipped through the cable stations, finally just leaving the television on Nickelodeon. Reruns of classic television shows were playing, and she found herself laughing along. Every so often she would check on Matt, and soon she found herself fighting to keep her eyelids from closing. Losing the battle, she drifted off to sleep as the clock ticked beyond midnight.

HE KNEW SHE'D MADE IT to his flat because the Saab he'd seen in her driveway was now parked in his normal spot. So she did drive that red convertible. Garrett glanced at his watch. He'd managed to get all the evidence on the case tonight, and arrests had been made. That had meant paperwork to complete.

Not that he was tired. Too much adrenaline and

caffeine still coursed through his veins. It would be a while before his nerves would calm and he'd be able to get some shut-eye. Which was okay, since tomorrow was Saturday and everyone could get some extra sleep.

He climbed up the stairs and used his key to unlock the back door. Only one light was on in the living room, and Garrett went through the kitchen, past the bathroom and through the dining area. Olivia was sound asleep on his couch.

She was beautiful, her dark hair falling over the throw pillow and covering one cheek. She was on her right side, and it was clear she'd fallen asleep while watching TV. He could almost picture the scene—she'd probably told herself that she'd close her eyes for only a minute. That minute had slipped into three, then five, until she'd fallen fast asleep. He hated to wake her. When he called her name, all he got was an "mmmph" as she covered her head with her arm.

He stood there, reluctant to touch her. The last thing he wanted was to wake her up and then have her drive home groggy. He didn't want her falling asleep behind the wheel. His father had handled those types of calls, and told of their often gruesome results.

Erring on the side of safety, Garrett left her sleeping and headed for the bathroom. After sitting in a car part of the night, then being out in a dusty old warehouse, he could use a shower to rinse off the grime. He glanced back at Olivia. He really knew nothing about all stages of sleep, but he felt it was best just to leave her for a little while longer.

OLIVIA AWOKE to the muted sound of running water. She blinked, taking a minute to remember exactly where she was. Then she remembered—she'd fallen asleep watching television at Garrett's. She blinked a few times. The room remained dark, except for the television and one side-table lamp. She peered around sleepily. Now the water had ceased running, and Olivia really didn't want to get off the couch and investigate further. Nothing had changed except the TV show. She'd fallen asleep to *Full House*; now an episode of *The Cosby Show* flickered on the screen.

Her head pounded and she shut her eyes again. She'd never been very good at shaking off sleep, especially after only a few hours. Since Garrett wasn't home, she'd just catch a few more winks. Luckily she didn't have to be anywhere on Saturday.

"Do you know you're a sight for sore eyes?" a deep male voice asked.

"I know my eyes are sore," Olivia said as she struggled to lift her eyelids again. Garrett *was* home. "I didn't hear you come in."

"I tried to be quiet."

She focused. Garrett wore a plain white T-shirt and blue jean cutoffs. His hair was damp, and the blond ends curled at his nape. "Did you take a shower? I thought I heard water."

"Yes, I did," Garrett admitted. He reached forward and moved a lock of her hair off her face. "Stakeouts are often messy and I'm covered in dirt when I get home. I can't stand it."

"Did you get him?"

"Who?" Garrett's forehead wrinkled.

"Whoever you were staking out," Olivia said with a wide yawn as she moved to a sitting position.

She'd blinked again, but those blue eyes of hers remained hypnotic. Garrett hesitated for a moment as he decided how to answer. Brenda couldn't have cared less about Garrett's job, so long as he brought home a paycheck—which of course had never been enough to satisfy her. Brenda had never wanted to hear what he did on his shift. But this was Olivia, and she was nothing like his ex-wife.

"We got him," Garrett said.

"Tell me about it," she said.

Garrett glanced down at her. Because of her position on the couch, her sweater had stretched and tightened over her breasts. Her blue eyes glimmered in the semi darkness, and her curiosity was evident.

"It wasn't very exciting." Garrett took a seat next to her. Her feet were bare and she tucked up her legs. "Time consuming, yes. We waited until he met the man he was trying to blackmail, recorded everything and moved in. He didn't try to resist arrest, so everything went down smoothly."

"And you're safe," Olivia said.

"We all were." Garrett said.

"Good. I worried about that," she said.

She had. When Garrett hadn't shown up, she'd begun to think of all the terrible things that could have happened to him. It had been a revealing experience;

she'd realized exactly how much she'd grown to care for this man in such a short period.

"I should probably get up. What time is it?"

"After two," Garrett said. "When did you fall asleep?"

"Midnight, maybe a little after," Olivia said. "Matt was in bed by eight. He was great. We went to McDonald's for dinner."

"Let me guess. You had a Big Mac."

"Wrong," Olivia said. "I had a grilled chicken caesar salad with a balsamic vinaigrette. I eat it to stay healthy, but it's actually good."

"You don't need to worry about your weight," Garrett said.

"Maybe not now," Olivia countered. "But I'm nine years away from forty."

"And I'm four," Garrett said. He stretched his neck by cocking his head to one side. "It's nothing to fear, really."

"You're a guy," she said. "Guys never have to worry."

"And just because you're a female means you should? You are the most beautiful women I've ever met, Olivia-who-never-called-me-back-this-week."

"Garrett."

His laugh was halfhearted. "I made the cardinal mistake, didn't I? I was one of those guys who come on way too strong, and the result is that the woman simply walks away. Maybe the challenge is gone—I don't know. But please tell me the truth."

"Maybe she's just afraid that she might hurt the guy," Olivia said. "She's not good at any of this relationship stuff and doesn't want to cause anyone any pain."

"I'm sure the guy's tough enough to handle things on his side," Garrett said with a soft smile. He reached forward and tucked Olivia's hair behind her left ear. "He's pretty solid."

That was good to hear.

"You know you fascinate me, don't you?" he asked. "I've jumped in way too fast, but somehow I couldn't help myself. And at this moment I definitely have to steal a kiss."

"Garrett, wait. I—I have something to tell you," she began.

His words made so much sense. Maybe she didn't have to run away. Maybe they could work through this. But to do that, she must tell him everything, before she chickened out and this moment slipped away.

Olivia Jacobsen wanted this man in her life. She didn't want to go away. She wanted to share her life, to be his partner.

Garrett wasn't a man who judged her; he didn't dominate her or seem to desire to change her. He completed her. If she told him the truth, what would be the result? Would he forgive her and still want her? Could he ever love her back?

She'd planned never to see him again after tonight, but exposing her secret was a risk she knew she must take. She had to roll the dice and see what numbers came up, then live with the results. Hopefully fate would be kind. He'd forgive her, and she could stay. For despite her earlier resolution to leave, staying was what she wanted more than anything. Priority number one—she had to tell him the truth.

But Garrett's mouth was close enough that she could feel his warm breath, making her confession like yesterday's news—easily forgotten, as her mind and body concentrated only on the magnetic proximity of this man she loved.

"It's time for a hello kiss," he whispered.

"A hello kiss?" she echoed.

He smiled, and she melted.

"The only proper way to greet a man when he comes home and you're lying on his couch."

"Oh," she said as his lips lowered to hers.

It was a kiss that started sweet and innocent but quickly roared into something bold and passionate. Their mouths molded together, and Olivia snaked her hands into his soft hair. This could be a hello kiss or, if he turned her away after her revelations, a goodbye kiss. For now, she'd take one more kiss.

And as Garrett moved his lips to her neck, Olivia knew she'd take one more night.

She'd been right about him all along. He was the man she loved with all her heart. He made her forget things like social status. Watching television on his couch, she'd found herself more at home than she was in her oversize pool house.

He made her relax. The tension she experienced

with him was sexual, not the worrisome, mental churning she had with others. She'd found nirvana in a man, a man she'd accepted exactly as is.

She'd nitpicked the flaws of all the other men in her life until now: like crooked teeth, for example, that annoyed her every time a guy opened his mouth, or the way he ate. She had found something wrong with every man she'd met, just so she had an excuse to end the relationship.

Garrett had flaws, but they hadn't bothered her. If anything, Garrett's imperfections made him perfect. She had no desire to change him.

She loved him.

Garrett's hand moved to cup a breast and Olivia shifted to allow him better access. She was bolder than she had been during her first effort at lovemaking, and placed her hands where they would give him the most pleasure. She was a quick learner.

"I'm awake now," she teased. Wide awake, wet and ready.

He stood and held out his arms. No words were spoken as he took her by the hand and led her to the bedroom. He locked the door behind him.

They made love in the darkness, quickly shedding the clothes that kept them physically apart. Garrett kissed her everywhere as he brought her to peak after peak with only his tongue.

She'd intended to touch him more, but he denied her, concentrating on her pleasure as he rained kisses and touches over her body. When she thought she could take no more, she heard a tiny rip as he protected himself and settled himself between her legs.

She'd tightened since the last time, and he stretched her as he drove deep, the still-new sensation of being entered registering in her consciousness, then vanishing as he began to move. Maybe someday she'd tell him he'd been her first lover, but that, too, became irrelevant as their bodies merged and began to take one path toward physical and mental completion.

She clung to him, kissing his lips and meeting his thrusts as he pushed them both over the edge. Afterward Garrett didn't roll away. Instead he shifted and drew Olivia close to his side.

"We have to stop not intending for this to happen," he said as he nipped her earlobe.

Olivia didn't answer. Already her tiredness was claiming her again, and Garrett's possessive arms had created an incredibly secure haven.

"I shouldn't be here in the morning," she said as sleep tiptoed in. "Besides, I still need to tell you—"

"Shh, it's fine," Garrett said. "Before Matt wakes up, I'll go crash on the couch. I refuse to let you drive this late when you're tired. Just go to sleep. I'd hate for anything to happen to you on the way home."

"I'd be fine," Olivia protested sleepily, her lie obvious as her eyelids fluttered down.

"Of course you would be," Garrett said, slipping away, "but I'm a cop and this way I won't have to worry."

She tried again. "I really need to tell you…"

But he had already escaped into the bathroom.

When he returned a few minutes later, he gathered her tightly into his arms. She'd never slept in a man's bed before, and she liked it. In fact, she loved it. She could stay here forever.

She'd make her confession and tell him everything in the morning, and maybe all would work out. She whispered a prayer before sleep claimed her. *Dear Lord, please let my life turn out fine. Just this once. I can live without learning about heartbreak. I promise I've changed and I won't hurt him.*

Let her be Mrs. Garrett Krause. That sounded so nice. Garrett was the man she could love for eternity and the man she could come home to. They'd work all the money issues out later. Yes, for once in her life, a relationship just might have a happy ending. She snuggled into his arms and entered a dreamless sleep.

Chapter Eleven

All hell broke loose the next morning at nine a.m. Garrett had moved to the couch over an hour ago, and Matt had slept in. In fact, everyone was still fast asleep when the front doorbell began to shrill.

Olivia jerked awake with surprise, the comforter dropping to her waist as she sat up. She glanced down and panicked. She'd slept naked! Where were her clothes? The bedroom door was safely closed, so she wrapped the comforter around herself and hobbled out of bed.

Everything she'd worn the night before was on the floor. Scared that Matt might enter and get a peek, Olivia used the bedspread for protection as she rapidly threw on her clothes.

The doorbell had ceased ringing. Still uncertain what was happening, Olivia opened the bedroom door. Garrett rushed by, stopping her exit. He wore only a pair of blue jean shorts. His torso was bare.

"Who is it?" she asked.

"Just stay there," he said, but it was already too late. A stunning redhead trotted on Garrett's heels, stopped short and gazed sharply at Olivia.

"Who the hell are you?" she asked, her green eyes sharp as she assessed the situation.

Olivia's stomach dropped to her toes. Never had she felt so conspicuous. Four-year-old Matt wouldn't have any idea what two consenting adults had done last night, but this woman could easily make the connection. Her angry expression indicated she'd guessed exactly what had transpired.

"You saw the blankets. You know I slept on the couch," Garrett told the woman. "Not that it's any of your business."

"My son should not be exposed to this…lifestyle," the woman said harshly. She began to push Matt's bedroom door open.

So this was the ex-wife. Her clothing was resort Lilly Pulitzer, a designer of choice for the St. Louis moneyed set. Olivia knew exactly what Clayton Road shop her outfit had come from. The ex-wife was perfectly put together, whereas Olivia was rumpled and unruly.

Garrett used his body to block Brenda's entrance to Matt's bedroom. "Good grief, Brenda. You're in no position to talk."

She planted her hands on her hips. "Garrett, if I'd known you were such a poor parental influence, I would have left the Hamptons sooner. And go put on a shirt."

Garrett held his anger in check. "You're a day early, and you're the one who had a half-dozen men before divorcing me and marrying one of them. That's no moral high ground from which to preach."

"Please. Irrelevant." Brenda gave an impatient wave of her hand. "You're a cop. You're supposed to be a father figure, not a philanderer. As for being early, technically this wasn't your weekend to have Matt. I was just being generous in giving you extra time. The Hamptons were hot, I was fed up and here I am. I want my son."

"*Our* son," Garrett corrected.

"Unfortunately," Brenda said. "But I love him dearly anyway."

Olivia winced at the charged exchange. So this was the infamous Brenda Krause, or whatever her married name was now. Brenda pushed the door open and walked to the bed, and Olivia observed Matt rubbing his eyes as he sat up. Unaware of any adult tension, Matt tossed his arms around his mother.

Then he glanced out the doorway and saw Olivia.

"Olivia's still here!" He wiggled out of Brenda's arms and stood atop his bed. "Hi, Olivia! Olivia's the greatest. She read me three bedtime stories while you were at work," he told his dad proudly.

Brenda turned around and fully studied Olivia. Brenda's green eyes narrowed. "Please tell me she isn't living here."

"I *want* Olivia to live here," Matt said, misinterpreting his mother's words. He clapped his hands once, and a panicked expression crossed his face. He then jumped off the bed and raced to the bathroom. The door closed behind him with a *click*.

An awkward silence descended.

"Olivia, meet Brenda," Garrett said. "My ex."

Brenda rose from her seat on the bed. "I'd say I was pleased to meet you, but I'm not happy with what I found here."

Garrett coughed, and Olivia could almost see him biting back a retort.

"Brenda, Matt wasn't exposed to anything," Garrett said. "Olivia babysat last night while I worked a stakeout. I slept on the couch and Olivia took the bed. I don't think you have any right to an opinion on my private life."

This time Brenda waved a hand as if swishing a fly, and Olivia could see that Brenda was a woman who did what she pleased, no matter whom it affected.

"Whatever, Garrett. This time I won't threaten you with any legal action."

Garrett frowned as Brenda continued, her voice dripping with sarcasm. "I must say, though, I'm very surprised at your choice of companions, especially her. So much for always swearing you wouldn't date anyone rich. Here you go again."

Garrett turned to Olivia, a confused expression on his face. Brenda saw it and dug deeper.

"Oh, please. This is too priceless. Didn't she tell you? You're Olivia Jacobsen, aren't you? I recognize you now. You haven't changed since high school."

Brenda shrugged. "We were in the play *Annie* together my senior year. I was Annie. Olivia had a minor role in the chorus. For some reason my parents donate to her father's ministry. They seem to think that donating will get them into heaven, but all they get are those silly family photos your father's ministry sends out at Christmas and a monthly newsletter saying how they can save the world. Gotta love my parents. They'll spend my inheritance on frivolity long before I get it."

Garrett crossed his arms and shifted his stance. "Brenda, leave Olivia out of this. This is not a conversation Matt should be exposed to, and a few minutes ago you said you were concerned about such things."

Brenda rolled her eyes. "Garrett, I knew you had someone here the moment I pulled up behind your car. Gwen doesn't drive a Saab. No one in this neighborhood can afford one."

"Did you ever think that maybe Gwen had company?"

"Please. She's half dead."

"Gwen could have had family visitors. And why does driving a Saab mean money?" Garrett asked. "They have great leases on automobiles these days."

"Your smoke screen is admirable, but for a detective, you are so clueless. Everyone knows Olivia Jacobsen goes through men like water.

"Not that I care who you date so long as it doesn't affect my son. If you want to buy your way onto easy street, then sleeping with the virginal Olivia Jacobsen might do it. Hmm, maybe you fixed that problem of hers. That'll make for an interesting follow-up to the column her mother wrote a few months ago. However, one warning, and only because I did care for you once. Be vigilant, because she dumps her fiancés pretty quickly. You may not get that free ride after all."

Olivia resisted the innate urge to say something to Brenda. Brenda was unreasonable, and there was no need to expose Matt to a cat fight.

"Brenda…" Garrett warned.

Brenda smirked. "Garrett, while I disapprove of your indiscretions around my son, the fact that you chose someone from my side of the tracks just cracks me up."

Now Garrett was staring at Olivia as if she had two heads, and Olivia inwardly cringed. Because he hadn't known the truth, he hadn't been able to stand his ground with Brenda. Instead, he'd found quicksand at his feet. Olivia winced. Being the brunt of his ex-wife's sarcasm had to be a blow to his ego, and Olivia had been the cause. By keeping Garrett in the dark, she'd taken away his ammunition and his chance to save face. He'd tried to do the chivalrous thing and defend her, but that had backfired. It was as if Olivia had stabbed him herself.

Before the conversation between the ex-spouses could continue, however, Matt chose that moment to exit the bathroom. He hopped on one foot and grinned widely as he approached. "I flushed, and I washed my hands."

"You're a good boy," Brenda said, her focus leaving Olivia as she moved Matt to the front door. "Come along, darling. Get dressed. I'm tired from my early-morning flight and I'm ready to go home."

Brenda barely glanced at Garrett as she reached for Matt's hand. "I'll swap clothes with you next week, Garrett. Just wash everything. I don't want to have to do laundry."

"Fine," Garrett said curtly.

Olivia went back into his bedroom and sat on the edge of the bed as Matt detached himself from Brenda and gave his dad a quick hug.

Tightness settled into Olivia's chest as Garrett and Brenda followed Matt into his room. This was one of the worst situations she had ever been in. She really had no idea what to do next.

As much as she'd like simply to grab her things and leave, this time she knew she couldn't just escape. She had to provide Garrett with an explanation. She'd just seen him badgered by his ex-wife, and it had been worse because Olivia had kept the truth from him.

Yes, she'd tried to tell him last night, but she hadn't tried strongly enough. She'd been selfish, thinking only of her own needs and desires. She'd fallen asleep.

Well, she'd gotten her "one more night," and she'd ruined everything in the process. As her future plans went up in smoke, Olivia knew that once again she'd have to keep her chin up and live with the poor decisions she'd made. She hadn't meant to hurt him, but had anyway.

She decided to make her excuses and leave the moment Matt and Brenda drove away. That took about five more minutes, and Olivia held back tears as Matt ran into Garrett's bedroom, wrapped his arms around her and hugged her tight.

"I love you, Olivia," he said.

Olivia smiled despite the fierce pain clawing at her soul. The crystal ball of the future was clear, and the picture wasn't pretty. She deserved whatever heart-break came her way, but that didn't lessen the intensity.

"Back at you, sport," she replied to Matt, her comment earning a scowl from Brenda and a stricken expression from Garrett. Olivia had to wipe away a tear as Matt tore out of the bedroom. She'd probably never see him again.

Moments later Olivia heard footsteps pounding down the stairs, and seconds later the front door slammed. Time to get ready to make her own exit. Her purse and shoes were still in the living room, and she went to retrieve them.

Garrett came back up the stairs then, and they were alone, standing in the living room.

Hollows had formed under his blue eyes. "We need to talk," he said.

Olivia gazed at her bare feet, and then she made the mistake of looking up. His expression contained anguish, disbelief, anger…she couldn't count the emotions. She'd caused each and every one. Guilt tore at her.

She had hurt the one she truly loved. It was one hundred percent her fault. Finally he spoke.

"From the moment we met, I knew you were a mystery, but I didn't know how much." Garrett folded his arms over his chest defensively.

He stared at her for a moment, and Olivia wanted to die from his scrutiny. Was this what a law breaker experienced—the overwhelming sense of despair and regret? Trying to find some balance, she shifted her weight. What could she say? How could she make this better?

The silence stretched, and at last Garrett went on, each word a knife. "Tell me, Olivia. Be honest if only for this once. Just how much of you is real and how much a lie?"

THE FLOOR still hadn't developed a hole that Olivia could drop through. Not that she believed God was going to answer Olivia's fervent prayer for escape. She glanced at the hardwood again, and when she gazed back up into Garrett's eyes, she was still in his living room and he was still furious.

"I never told any outright lies," Olivia said slowly, her mind racing as she tried to find a way to explain. Even if the relationship died, she had to clear up any misunderstandings. "What I did was to fail to correct some of your assumptions. I planned on telling you everything last night."

Garrett's eyebrows arched in disbelief. "Before or after we had sex?" he asked sharply.

Olivia's knees locked. "Before," she managed to say. Some of her confidence returned as she went on. "Remember? I said I had things to tell you."

"You may have told me that," he said. He rolled his shoulders to ease some tension. "But it's irrelevant. You lied, Olivia. By omission or outrightly, you didn't tell the truth."

"No," she admitted.

His expression grew more stricken. "You know how I feel about the truth. How honesty is the most important thing. How many weeks did you have to come clean?"

"You only needed one date," Olivia said, pleading with him to understand. "You were the one who assumed I was a counter girl. I didn't even know what you did for a living at that point. But I wanted one date with you. So I took it and let you think what you did about my occupation."

"Why?" He crossed his arms again.

He had not put on a shirt, and she swallowed. "Why what?"

"Why did *you* only want one date?"

Olivia shut her eyes. This was so horrible. How could she ever have thought losing her virginity in a one-night stand was a good idea? Bad girls had bad ideas.

"The truth," he demanded.

Her eyes flew open. "I…"

"Did you plan to seduce me?" The question was a harsh accusation.

Olivia tapped her foot. "The thought entered my mind. I wasn't searching for you. I'd left work that day with a lot on my mind. You showed up at the counter and *your* problem seemed like an answer to *my* problem."

"What problem?"

"The one Brenda mentioned."

Garrett's face froze. A professional poker player couldn't have been more unreadable. "The virginal Olivia Jacobsen."

Olivia again lowered her gaze. This was not how she'd envisioned her revelation. What she'd done was out there now, and it rang tawdry. Which was exactly how Garrett took it.

"Is that it? Did I guess? I needed one date, you needed one night. As you said, you didn't even know my last name. You just wanted a quick lay."

"When I was behind the counter, it seemed like a good idea." Olivia said. She glanced back up then and somehow met his accusing eyes. "But it wasn't. I didn't expect you to call. And then you did, and we played a little game. Admit it."

"Okay." Garrett conceded that one point.

"And then I got to know you and you received a page and dinner ended. And I did want to get to know you better so…"

"It made you feel less guilty when you seduced me later that night."

"Yes. No." She tossed her hands in the air. His words were so harsh, so bitter. "If anything, I felt worse. I was raised that sex is something special. And maybe I'm inexperienced—okay, I am—but to me that one moment was special. But you just left and I went to bed alone. And then you didn't call. If anything, I learned that a one-night stand isn't all it's cracked up to be."

He scowled. "Bully for you. You found a stud you could use. In reality, you were probably relieved that I didn't call. You got what you wanted. If it didn't live up to your expectations, that's not my fault. Whatever mental baggage you have is your problem. I've got enough going on in my own life."

"I discovered I cared for you. I'm terrible with men. My history scared me. I always hurt someone. As I'm hurting you right now. I'm botching things up, and no matter how sorry I am, I can't make them better."

"You know, Cliff tried to warn me about you. But he held his tongue."

"I was engaged to his cousin Austin."

Disbelief flickered, then disgust took over. "Engaged?"

Olivia winced. More nails in her coffin. "I've been engaged twice, neither time for very long. My longest steady relationship lasted fourteen months, and I wasn't ever engaged to him." She paused. "No one's ever made me feel the way you have."

He shook his head and snorted cynically. "That's only because we had sex. Please, Olivia, I'm jaded. Do you know how many women have said that to me? Ever heard of the Hometown Heroes charity calendar?"

"Chrissy had it."

He frowned. "Who's Chrissy?"

"She's my friend who does work the *Monitor*

counter. She was in the bathroom when you arrived. She showed me the page you're on."

"Before or after I left?"

"After. I'd never seen it," Olivia said. He seemed skeptical. "That's the truth, believe it or not."

"I'm not sure I do," Garrett said. "It's because of that calendar that I had women dropping by my work and mailing me letters. The things they sent and said were outrageous. Offers of marriage, endless sex and no strings. I'm not that type of guy. Despite my divorce, I value commitment. I think long term, not immediate moment. You're the antithesis of all I value."

"No, I'm really not. But I'm turning thirty-one. My behavior was a momentary aberration. Haven't you ever been simply unhappy and desperate enough to do anything to change it?"

"Yeah, before I divorced my unfaithful, dishonest wife."

At that moment, as if timed, Garrett's pager went off. He'd left it on the coffee table. Now he strode over and glanced at it. He frowned, then grabbed his cell phone and dialed.

"Yeah, what's up?"

Garrett listened, and Olivia saw his face whiten.

"You're kidding me. No, this did not happen. I don't need this news today. This has to be a joke." He paused, clearly stricken. "Yes, I'll be right there. Give me five minutes to get on my way." Garrett closed the flip phone.

"What's wrong?" Olivia asked.

"I don't have time for this anymore," Garrett said,

his attention already on whatever bad news that call had been. "Do me a favor and show yourself out."

"Garrett," she said. "Garrett, I do care for you." He was truly through with her, and panic unlike she'd ever known consumed her.

"Olivia!" Garrett snapped, and something in his demeanor worried her. "If you care for me, then prove it. Leave."

"Okay, I'm going." Olivia put her feet into her sandals and grabbed her purse. Garrett remained unmoving as Olivia made her way down the back stairs and out to her car. She slid into the Saab and put the key in the ignition. The car started immediately, and she made a left on Kingshighway.

She would not cry. Refused to cry. She bit her lip to keep the tears from flowing. She'd listen to the radio. Hearing someone talk would keep her mind off how badly she'd mucked this up.

She'd reached Southwest Avenue when KMOX radio personalities returned after a commercial break. Their show was almost finished for the morning, and they jumped onto the top news story of the day.

Still shaken from her blunt dismissal, she needed a minute for what they were saying to register.

"Unbelievable that they'd both be police officers," the male newscaster said.

"I know. What is the coincidence in that?" the female newscaster said.

Olivia increased the radio volume.

"For those of you just joining us this morning,

we've been discussing a fatal accident that happened last night on Highway 44 involving two police officers. The only information that has been released is that off-duty officer Elmer Fuchs was traveling westbound in an eastbound lane and hit officer Pete Shepard head-on near Antire Road. Shepard had been out investigating a lead.

"The area was under a heavy layer of fog at the time, and weather may have been a factor in the accident," the female newscaster added. "Funeral arrangements are incomplete at this time, but contributions can be made to the BackStoppers. Officer Shepard is survived by his wife Moira, their grown children and several grandchildren. We don't have any information on Officer Fuchs's family yet.

"Stay tuned to KMOX throughout the day for more information at the top of this hour. For KMOX, this is…"

As the radio personalities signed off, Olivia attempted to loosen her hold on the steering wheel. She'd unconsciously gripped it as tightly as she could. She pressed the button that shut off the radio, then cut over at Hampton and within minutes had entered westbound Highway 40.

Dear God. Garrett's page had been about the accident. Moira's husband…Pete, who had laughed jovially yet made Olivia comfortable about her pathetic attempt at playing washers…Moira's husband was dead. Poor Moira, who had welcomed Olivia with open arms.

Tears began to flow and this time Olivia couldn't stop them. They ran down her face in rivers, a reminder of her guilt, her pain and her helplessness. Poor Garrett. The man she loved hurt—because of her, and now because of this.

And there was nothing she could do. No comfort could she give. If she cared, she'd go away as he'd asked.

The problem was, she cared too much and couldn't go away.

Olivia exited north at Lindbergh, made a quick right at Conway and another quick left on South Warson. Less than three minutes later, she made a right turn onto Ladue Road, and less than two minutes after that she turned right onto her street. She didn't head straight to the pool house, though, instead, she entered the main gates and parked in the large circular drive of her parents' house. She used her key and headed straight toward the solarium, where her parents often breakfasted.

As she approached the open French doors, she could see one gray head over the back of the wingback chair. She dropped her purse onto the terrazzo floor and ran into the room. Amazingly, Sara wasn't there. "Dad?"

Blake Jacobsen moved his coffee cup and placed his Bible on a nearby table. Maybe it was the frantic tone of her voice, but instinct had him rising and opening his arms as his youngest daughter flew into them. Tears still ran down her face.

"Dad," Olivia said. "I have something to tell you."

Chapter Twelve

"Moira?" Trisha Wunderlich said as she entered Moira's living room. Since the tragic announcement, Trisha, Moira's best friend, had arrived and taken over. The Shepard house was an old Victorian in Webster Groves, and the mid-size room was crowded with family and police officers.

Most had arrived as soon as they heard the news. Garrett had come, as had Ben, Mason and Cliff—Pete's colleagues and Friday night poker buddies. Moira had hugged each of them and whispered how grateful she was that they'd shown.

No one wanted to leave Moira alone. They wanted to be there, and somehow by all being there, they were able to wordlessly communicate their grief and disbelief that this had happened. Pete Shepard, so close to retirement—so suddenly gone.

Oh, it was always in the back of the mind of every police officer's wife that her husband could be killed while on duty. She worried, whether she acknowledged her fear or not. But no cop's wife expected her husband to die being hit head-on by an off-duty cop driving in the wrong lane. Pete had been out working a lead, a routine event. That he hadn't returned from his shift was surreal.

"Moira?" Trisha said again. "Moira, you have visitors. Blake Jacobsen and Chief Andrew Goebel are here to see you."

As Garrett heard the names, his head shot up. The BackStoppers had arrived. They were a St. Louis organization devoted to serving the families of police officers and firefighters who had died in the line of duty. Since 1959, the BackStoppers had had but one purpose: to provide assistance for the spouses and dependent children. Usually arriving within hours of a tragedy, the organization provided immediate money, which was often used to cover funeral expenses.

"I didn't know Blake Jacobsen was a BackStopper," Garrett said to Ben.

"He's on their board of directors," Ben replied. He was the type of man who knew about such things. He was also a genius at trivia. Pete had often joked that Ben should try out for *Jeopardy*.

Garrett watched Jacobsen and Chief Goebel enter the room. Even though Chief Goebel worked for the fire department, Garrett had met him previously. It was the taller man next to him who interested Garrett, and as the crowd in the living room began to move to the kitchen, Garrett lingered a minute to get his first glimpse of Olivia's father.

In his sixties, Blake was still the kind of man who filled doorways. He was easily as tall as Garrett, and the suit he wore made him seem paternal rather than formal. Crows-feet and heavy lines etched his face, but his expression was gentle and kind. He exuded an inner peace that seemed to bring immediate comfort to those in the room, and even Moira looked more settled as the man many people referred to as God's servant entered.

The thing that really struck Garrett, though, was Blake Jacobsen's eyes. Garrett had seen those eyes before—on Olivia. They weren't exactly the same, but that outer ring of darker blue was similar. Blake sensed Garrett's scrutiny and turned, and for a moment Garrett froze. Blake's expression never changed. He didn't judge, yet clearly he might have been speaking. Blake knew.

As THE LAST MAN exited the living room, Blake Jacobsen turned to Moira Shepard. He'd been working with the BackStoppers for years now, but never had his daughter come to him and requested his involvement.

Olivia had been quite upset this morning when she arrived home. That morning had been rare because Sara hadn't been home. She'd left early to babysit for Shane and Lindy. This had given Blake his first opportunity in a long time to talk with his daughter. She'd confessed everything.

He hadn't been shocked, only surprised that what she'd done hadn't happened sooner. But love was like that. When you weren't searching for it, that was when it found you. Olivia hadn't been out searching for love; she'd only wanted a fling.

But she'd fallen, and hard. She loved a defender of the public trust, a man who at this moment was probably pacing the Shepard kitchen, wishing he could do more, wishing he could somehow turn back time and stop Pete from making that fateful drive.

God's ways often weren't anything man could comprehend. Man had to rely on faith, and therein lay the problem. Mankind wanted scientific explanations. God's way provided few answers. Faith was the realization that the answer to "why" might never be found.

As for Olivia, she would have to make her own path. In the split second he'd seen Garrett, Blake had sensed honor and integrity in Garrett Krause. His daughter had described him well, but this was understandable. How many relationships started with passion, then become true love? The majority, Blake knew. It only took time and patience—and faith.

Olivia's road wouldn't be easy, but this morning she hadn't been thinking of herself. She had been concerned only for Moira, and what Olivia's father could do to help. For a moment Blake had been young again, taken back to a time when his five-year-old daughter thought her father was a hero and believed he could save the world. But Blake knew he could only work through Him who gave him strength.

Now he opened his Bible and sat down next to Moira. Even though years had passed since he'd lost

Kristina, moments like these brought his first wife's death back and deepened his compassion and empathy. He placed his hand over Moira's. "Let us pray."

"SO WHAT DO YOU THINK of him?"

Garrett turned. Cliff stood leaning against the countertop. "I'm glad the BackStoppers are here," Garrett said. "I didn't realize they moved so fast."

"Same day," Cliff said. "They provide immediate support and assistance, then come back in two weeks, once the initial shock is over. So you do know that's Olivia's father in there?"

"Yes," Garrett said. The information had stung, but had quickly been overshadowed by the depth of emotion he was feeling over Cliff's death.

Real men weren't supposed to cry, but every man in that kitchen knew that when he found himself in private, the tears would flow. Now, being strong for Moira was all that mattered, and the more of them who were in the group, the easier it was to pretend they were all John Wayne tough.

So if Cliff wanted to discuss Olivia, that was fine with Garrett. Discussing her gave him something else to be angry about, something he could control. Pete's death couldn't be undone, and Garrett's anger boiled over the accident. Even in the fog, how could one cop crash into another? Cops were trained to drive under all sorts of harsh conditions. Why Pete, and why now, when he had been so close to retirement? The questions had no answers, and to keep spinning one's wheels and grasping for explanations would drive a man insane.

"So you understand what I was trying to tell you?" Cliff asked.

"Yeah. You were trying not to reveal everything, because that wasn't your place. Instead, you warned me, which is your place."

"It was tough," Cliff admitted. "I'm your friend. I care."

"I know. But the brutal thing was having Brenda show up early this morning and demand Matt back. She didn't take too kindly to Olivia's presence. However, it's not something she'll have to worry about again."

"You aren't going to see Olivia anymore?" Cliff asked. Someone handed Cliff a cup of coffee, and before moving away, the officer glanced at Garrett.

"No." Garrett shook his head, his answer doing double duty. The man moved off and Garrett returned his attention to Cliff. "No, I'm not going to see Olivia again. The timing isn't conducive to having any kind of relationship, especially with Pete gone."

"Okay," Cliff said slowly. He straightened and took a sip of coffee. "And you told her this?"

"She's pretty much got it figured out," Garrett said.

Cliff gave a low whistle. "That sounds rough. Things didn't end well, then?"

"You should be delighted to hear that, and at this moment do me a favor and drop it," Garrett said. He might have had an earlier desire to talk, but he'd changed his mind. Making love with Olivia last night had been heaven. He'd held her close all night, before moving to the couch early in the morning. He'd fallen back to sleep quickly, dreaming of the future—and woken up in hell.

TIME PASSED SLOWLY over the next few weeks, as well. The funeral had been a moving and emotional experience. Pete had been an army veteran, and so had been interred in Jefferson Barracks National Cemetery. He'd received a twenty-one-gun salute, and Moira had received the folded-up American flag that had covered his coffin.

Blake Jacobsen had officiated at the graveside service, and Garrett had found his words moving. Most people had shaken the minister's hand on their way to say final condolences to Moira, and Garrett had been no exception.

But after shaking Garrett's hand, Blake had done a strange thing. He'd reached out and placed his hand squarely on Garrett's shoulder. Eyes so similar to Olivia's had radiated understanding. "You're a good man for caring, Garrett," Blake had said, and then he'd released and turned his attention to the next person in line.

The brief encounter had left Garrett shaken, and he found himself online that evening discovering everything he could about Blake Jacobsen and his evangelical ministry. Property tax records revealed Olivia lived in her parents' pool house, and that the entire estate had been a gift from her grandparents to her parents.

He'd learned that Blake had turned down a role in the family company, choosing to build a ministry, instead. Olivia's father didn't need money, and all donations sent to the ministry were channeled to charities that helped the poor and needy. Unlike the 2005 scandal that had plagued another St. Louis-based ministry, Blake Jacobsen was squeaky clean and deservedly so. The man had prayed with kings and presidents, and while he'd often officiated at funerals for fallen officers, in Pete's case he'd postponed a trip to South America to do the funeral. It had meant the world to Moira.

There could be only one reason he'd taken such an interest. If Blake knew who Garrett was, that meant Olivia had said something to her father.

Olivia remained a contradiction and one he'd been unable to forget since Pete's death. Garrett had dissected the reason for his behavior from every angle, but each time he'd only ended up frustrated. The reason couldn't be love—they'd barely gotten started on the relationship. There was no way he'd fallen for Olivia Jacobsen.

Besides, he didn't rush. He'd made that mistake with Brenda, and everything had fallen apart quickly. He paused a moment as a heated memory claimed him. He *had* jumped into things with Olivia. They went to bed on the night of their first date. And he was right back in bed with her the third time they were together.

What had it been about Olivia that had drawn him, made him yearn to be with her despite all her contradictions? He'd suspected, from the beginning, that she wasn't what she appeared to be, but it hadn't mattered. Had his soul known something his head and heart hadn't?

Blake Jacobsen had uttered the truth: Garrett cared especially for Olivia. A lot. He'd let her meet Matt, something he'd never allowed with any other woman post-Brenda. He'd brought Olivia to his house, something else he'd never done. He had let her get underneath his skin and into his life.

Garrett sighed and shut down his work computer. Whatever had been between them didn't matter now. One couldn't erase time or undo the ugliness that had occurred. Sometimes silence was the best apology.

Hopefully in this case, it would do.

"I'm WORRIED About Garrett," Ben said. It was September fifteenth, and he, Mason and Cliff were sitting having a beer in Dogtown after their shift. "He's not been the same since Pete died."

"None of us has," Cliff said. No one had any desire to play Friday-night poker anymore, so instead they hung out drinking. Not necessarily a better option, although they all made sure they were sober before driving anywhere or took a taxi.

Following Pete's death, their tight-knit group had survived but hadn't totally recovered. A month had passed since the funeral, but they still were adrift.

Moira's sister had arrived and moved in, so their visits to Moira had fallen off. Trisha Wunderlich had said that the men reminded Moira of Pete, and they'd respectfully given Moira the space she needed.

Life went on; that was one thing everyone had learned from Pete's death. But Ben was accurate: Garrett hadn't recovered. Garrett was not only smarting from Pete's death, but he'd broken off with Olivia.

As much as Cliff would have liked to believe that was a good thing, he was beginning to have second doubts. Garrett had never acted this way. He'd become totally withdrawn, focusing only on work and Matt. Instead of being out tonight with the guys, Garrett had gone home, where he would have only the television as company.

"So what's this that I hear about some bachelor auction?" Mason asked, breaking the silence. "When is it? Two weeks?"

"Yeah, and it's for BackStoppers," Cliff said. "I've been roped into it. I'm not sure whose idea it was, but it's been in the works for a while, since before Pete's death."

"But the event wasn't going anywhere," Mason said. "Organizers thought they'd have to cancel."

"It really got off the ground when Jacobsen Enterprises and its restaurant, Grandpa Joe's Good Eats, agreed to underwrite the event the Monday after Pete's passing. The money really let that women's charity group get to work."

"Pete loved Grandpa Joe's and those pellers they make," Mason said, mentioning the chili-and-egg combination the restaurant was known for.

"Anything earned is pure profit for BackStoppers," Cliff finished. The announcement had come as a complete shock to the organizers, but they'd been thrilled when Joe Jacobsen called and made the offer.

"I haven't been asked yet," Ben said. "Then again, what type of women bid on these things?"

"Rich women," Mason said. "I got my invite to participate today."

"I could use a rich woman," Ben joked. His marriage to his dream woman was four months away, and he knew engaged men weren't on the program. "When is it?"

"In two weeks, on September twenty-ninth. They've lined up most of the eligible guys from the calendar, and now they're after anyone else they can get."

"Garrett agreed?" Ben arched an eyebrow.

"Garrett agreed," Cliff said. "I think it had more to do with an obligation to Pete's memory—after all, the BackStoppers have really helped Moira. Trisha Wunderlich approached him personally."

"True," Mason said. "I'm just surprised he'd agree since he was adamant he'd never again do anything that invaded his privacy."

"It's only one night, one date," Cliff said.

"Boy, does that sound familiar," Ben said.

Cliff lifted his longneck beer to his lips. "Yeah," he said finally. "I guess it does."

"I'M NOT SURE how you talked me into going to the bachelor auction," Olivia said as she refolded her napkin and placed it in her lap. She was wearing a simple yellow two-piece outfit, nothing fancy at all, but she didn't want food stains on it. So since she didn't have to go home in between work and the auction, she'd met her grandfather for dinner.

"I guess I should be grateful that Claire will be there, too. You know how much I hate these things," she said.

"What—a bunch of women screaming and shelling out big bucks for charity?" Grandpa Joe said, a twinkle in those eyes so like Olivia's.

"It still seems degrading to watch a bunch of men prance around," Olivia said. "Remember, it was Claire's idea to do that charity calendar and this event, not mine. She's in that group that organizes events and donates the money to whatever charity they see fit. She could go in my place, instead of with me."

"Aw, lighten up a little," her grandfather teased. "That's your upbringing talking. Claire's excited about tonight, and you two haven't done anything together lately. It's fun and for a good cause, and no one got blackmailed into participating. Besides, I heard some Blues and Rams players are participating. Those guys should go for top dollar. The event sold out in the first forty-eight hours."

Olivia forked a bite of her chicken piccata. She and Claire would head over to the Millennium Hotel's Grand Ballroom in about a half hour. The doors opened at seven-thirty, with the first man up for bid at eight-thirty. The speeches to start the event began at eight-fifteen, which was the part Olivia was involved in. "I don't even know who's in the auction or up for bid. I didn't see a program."

"Oh, the auction committee has it. You can get one when you arrive. Don't worry. All you really have to do is be there and give a short speech."

Olivia tried again. "Couldn't Claire have done this?"

"Nope," Grandpa Joe said with a grin. "You get to take the acknowledgment for Jacobsen Enterprises and Grandpa Joe's Good Eats. You *are* Jacobsen's vice president of corporate communications, our number-one PR person. Although Claire did all the prep work for us, as your CEO, I say it's your job now."

"Not for much longer," Olivia said. "I'm seriously considering that position with O'Brien Publications. I'm thirty-one now—have been for two weeks—and I'm after new challenges. It's probably past time to move on and get out from under Sara's thumb."

"You might be right," Grandpa Joe said. "At least in New York she can't keep putting you in her ministry column. When do you fly out and meet with Cameron?"

"We agreed to discuss the appointment next Friday, now that the announcement is official," she said. "They've moved their timeline back a little. The job wasn't to start until mid-November instead of sometime in October. I thought I'd take the following week off so I could see some theater, visit some museums and scout out the city."

"A good idea," Grandpa Joe said. "So how's that guy you were seeing? What's he think of all this?"

"I'm not," Olivia said sharply. "So he isn't involved. We broke off over four weeks ago."

"Oh," Grandpa Joe said quietly. "I'm sorry to hear that." He lifted his fork and took a bite of grilled salmon. "I just love Henrietta's salmon."

"I agree," Olivia said. Named after Grandpa Joe's wife, Henrietta's was one of the few five-star, five-diamond restaurants in the nation. Olivia's sister Claire managed it. Olivia had figured meeting her grandfather for dinner here was better than going home to microwavable food at the pool house.

Her parents had left for South America the day after Pete's funeral, missing Olivia's birthday, though they'd called and wished her well. Her parents never had been good about celebrating birthdays once the children were past high school. In fact, her father had forgotten to call Shane and wish him a happy twenty-fifth birthday, which had truly been a slight because Shane and Blake shared the same birth date.

Olivia had turned thirty-one alone, but that wasn't necessarily a bad thing. It had given her time to think, and plan. She'd also used the time to try to file Garrett away as only a memory. She hadn't been as successful as she could have liked, but she'd made progress.

As for her twin, Nick had spent his birthday with Maxie in Chicago. Olivia had called Nick and talked to him for a while, but by the end of the conversation he still hadn't told her he was getting married. The next Monday, Grandpa Joe told Olivia that Nick and Maxie had decided to tell everyone about their engagement at Thanksgiving, and were planning an intimate wedding for the following June. That Blake and Sara were also oblivious to their son's engagement made Olivia's disappointment a little more palatable. Nick was keeping his news from everyone.

"So what happened?" Grandpa Joe asked casually.

Olivia stopped pushing pieces of the chicken piccata around. She set her fork down. Had she been daydreaming? "What?"

"What happened with the guy?"

"It didn't work out," Olivia said. "And a friend of his died. Now is not the best time for either of us to have a relationship."

"But you liked him?"

Olivia felt as though she'd been stabbed in the heart. She still loved him. "A great deal," she replied honestly.

"And you don't think there's any hope?" Grandpa Joe reached for his iced tea and took a long sip. He appeared troubled.

Olivia shook her head. She'd worn her hair straight down with curl at the ends. "No. Besides, I'll probably be moving."

"Oh," Grandpa Joe said, placing his glass back on the table. "So, were you planning on going to any World Series games?"

"Maybe if the Cardinals get that far," she said,

grateful for the new topic of conversation. Her pain over Garrett and how badly she'd blown it with her lies was still too raw.

"Oh, the Cardinals will," Grandpa Joe said. "You just watch."

As they moved to less sensitive topics, Olivia and her grandfather finished dinner without any further mention of her romance troubles.

When they had finished, Claire approached the table. "Are you ready?" Since the doors opened at seven-thirty, Claire meant to leave by seven-twenty. Olivia and her sister could have walked the distance safely, but it would be midnight before the benefit ended, and Claire had offered to drive.

Olivia had always admired her older sister. Claire was thirty-three and too busy to worry about the fact that she wasn't married. Claire's every moment was full: she managed Henrietta's; she had authored two cookbooks, including one James Beard award winner; she served on the boards of five charitable organizations. Whereas Olivia worried about being an old maid, Claire was comfortable in her skin, refused to compromise and hadn't met anyone who accepted her "as is."

Like Olivia, Claire had the Jacobsen blue eyes. But black was her color, and now she wore black pants and a black sequined top that shimmered and highlighted Claire's slender figure.

Olivia rose, already feeling a bit overshadowed by her older sister. Claire's dark hair was cropped short in the latest style, and Olivia wished she'd done something more with hers. She also wished she wasn't wearing only a simple yellow outfit and matching sandals. Maybe she should have gone for the glamour, like her sister.

"You're fine," Claire said, reading Olivia's mind as they walked to Claire's big indulgence, her new Corvette convertible. "Relax. You look great. What matters is not what you're wearing but how big a check you can write."

"I wasn't planning on bidding," Olivia said. "I have to do my part of the program at eight-fifteen, and then I'm done. I could leave before the first man is up for bid at eight-thirty."

"But you won't, because you're on a girls' night with me and we haven't done one of these in forever. So bring your wallet just in case," Claire said. "I'm bringing mine. A woman should always be prepared to spend money if she sees something she likes."

Claire drove in through the valet entrance of the Millennium at exactly seven-thirty. She handed over her keys to the eager valet, shooting him a forceful "there's a huge tip waiting for you if there's not one scratch on it when I get it back" expression.

Claire watched as the valet departed with her car, sighing as if turning her baby over had been very difficult. "Ready?" she said to Olivia.

"I'm coming," Olivia replied. She wobbled once on her one-inch pumps. Why was she so nervous? She'd handled bigger PR events. Here, she would walk on stage, walk off. If she got desperate and didn't wish to stay, she could have the doorman call a cab and be driven back to her car, which she'd left at Henrietta's.

As they approached the queue of people outside the grand ballroom, Olivia swallowed. Everyone was dressed to the nines in black. Jewelry, sequined gowns and beaded purses all glittered, and updo hairstyles were the rage. Olivia felt like a plain Jane.

"We're supposed to use a side entrance," Claire said. "We're part of the event. It's this way."

She led Olivia down a side hallway, and soon they were inside the ballroom. Claire dropped Olivia off with the event coordinator, who had some last-minute instructions for her on how the auction would begin and what Olivia should say. Before Olivia knew it, Claire had returned.

"It's time to find our seats."

"It's starting already?" Olivia asked.

"Yes. I got you a program and a number in case you'd like to make a bid. You can glance at the program once you're done speaking," Claire said.

"You registered me?" Olivia asked. "I'm not bidding."

"You might change your mind. I have. I'm going to bid on that single Rams player. You know, the kicker who's new to the team this year."

Olivia understood who Claire meant. Ever since training camp the media had been going gaga over the Rams' newest player and his potential. "He's eight years younger than you," Olivia pointed out.

"So?" Claire said with a shrug. "I never go for older men. Now, go do your stuff."

The opening ceremony went well. Once in her element, Olivia projected confidence as she acknowledged Jacobsen Enterprises's role in underwriting the event. Attitude really made the outfit, she knew, and she was a Jacobsen. With applause ringing in her ears, she returned to her seat.

At least fifty men were up for bid tonight, and they'd been randomly divided into groups of five. Olivia flipped idly through the program. Like a theater program, most of the pages consisted of ads. Toward the center, the charity brochure had small pictures and short bios of each man, five to a page. Olivia had read one spread before the auctioneer came onstage and the actual bidding started. She closed the program and stuck it under her seat.

Because of her and her sister's positions with the committee, they had front row seats. Olivia had a good view of the first five men who moved onstage. They included three firefighters, one banker and one professional chef. Olivia sighed her relief. No men in just pants and bow ties here. She had let her romance-novel imagination run away with her. As if anything donating money to BackStoppers would have half-naked men running around. All the men wore complete tuxes that had been donated for the event.

The women went wild, especially for one of the guys who had been in that Hometown Heroes calendar. Bidding for him was spirited, and as he let loose a cheeky grin, Olivia could see why. Even Claire had to bid, although once overbid, she kept her number down.

"What?" Claire said as she flashed Olivia a sheepish grin. "I'm still after the kicker. For a moment I just got carried away. He is cute. You should have seen him model during the calendar shoot. There are perks for serving on charity boards, you know."

The first group brought in a little over six thousand dollars, and Claire seemed pleased. "We made over one hundred fifty thousand on tickets alone. We also get a cut on the bar. This is going to be a great night."

"Congratulations," Olivia said. "So you're more involved in this than I thought."

"Not really. While I'm part of the group, this wasn't really my event. I'm too busy working on next year's calendar. We start selling in just a few weeks."

"Oh, okay." Olivia stifled a yawn. She'd had an early meeting, and she was tired. The room was also hot, as if the air-conditioning hadn't kicked on in a while. Maybe it was just because she was close to the heavy stage lights. She retrieved her program from under her seat and fanned her face with it for a moment, and then opened it to check out the next group.

"After we do the auction, we'll all be able to meet our men," Claire said as she ordered a glass of wine from a roving waitress. "Do you want anything to drink?"

Actually, something cold sounded good. "Could you bring me a diet cola?" Olivia asked.

"Sure," the waitress said. She wrote the order down before she left.

Claire arched an eyebrow. "No wine?"

"No," Olivia said. "And the soda will have caffeine. I'm a bit run-down."

"Oh." Claire directed her attention back to the stage.

Olivia glanced up for a moment. A personal trainer was the subject of the current heated bid. She flipped the page to see and frowned.

"What's he doing in here?"

"Who?" Claire leaned over to study the left-hand page. "Cliff Jones. Hmm, he's not too bad. Says he's a cop, which would be why he's here. A lot of police and firefighters agreed to be auctioned off."

"He's Austin's cousin," Olivia said.

"Well, his side of the family got all the looks," Claire said, nodding approvingly at Cliff's photo.

Olivia grimaced. Claire had never been very impressed with Austin.

"Does he have money, too?" Claire asked.

"I think so," Olivia said, remembering what Moira had told her at the picnic. "He went to J. B. High School."

"Then maybe I should bid on him. I'll have to see when he gets onstage."

"You're bidding on the football player," Olivia pointed out.

Claire grinned. "Who says I can't bid on two men? My royalty check arrived. I'm flush."

Olivia rolled her eyes and giggled. "Sara would kill you."

"Aw, let her," Claire said. "She doesn't scare me. You do know that I threatened never to visit the house if she put me in any of her columns again."

Olivia's eyes widened. "You didn't."

"Of course I did. Why else did she stop mentioning me? Really, Olivia, from here on out, as your big sister, I command you to live your own life. Stop stressing over what Sara thinks. If you see something you want, go for it and stop worrying whether it's proper. The family survived Shane's antics. They can survive yours, too, so make some."

"I tried. It didn't work out," Olivia said. Garrett was perfect proof of that.

Claire's eyes narrowed with determination. "Well, dust yourself off and try again. Tonight, promise me that if you like someone, you'll go for him."

"Sure," Olivia said. Like there was a chance of that. After all, the man she wanted was no longer available, and no bevy of men for sale would change that. "I promise."

Claire twisted her head sharply, as if to see if Olivia was serious. "Good. I'm holding you to that."

"Whatever," Olivia said as the next round of guys entered the room and took the stage. She gave them a once-over. There was a disk jockey from a local radio station, an investment banker, an emergency medical technician, an entrepreneur and Cliff Jones. Not one of them appealed to her. Going for something she wanted was not a promise she'd have to fret about keeping.

"Not one?" Claire said.

"No," Olivia said.

"Maybe you should turn some more pages," Claire said, "while I bid on Cliff."

"He's older than you," Olivia said.

"So? Nothing says I can't try an older man now and then," Claire replied. She watched as the first man went up for bid. "Plus he's got money. I'm tired of men being after me for mine."

Olivia sighed. Garrett hadn't wanted her because she had money. She'd been *too* rich, too like his ex-wife. The waitress brought their drinks, and Olivia set the program down. Bidding began on the third man. Cliff was last in the current lineup.

"Are you going to read that program or not?" Claire said. "You really should be prepared."

Frustration obvious, Olivia exhaled. "Prepared for what? I told you that if I saw someone I liked, I'd bid."

Claire grabbed her own program. "You know, Olivia, I love you. You are blissfully naive and clueless, whereas I am worldly and knowledgeable. Sometimes I envy you and your innocence, and wish I could be more like you, but not tonight. Can't you smell a setup?"

"Setup?" Olivia blinked.

Claire opened the program and plopped it in Olivia's lap. "Remember, you promised to bid on someone you wanted."

"Wait. You're telling me that Grandpa Joe insisted that I represent Jacobsen Enterprises tonight so I could buy a man?"

Claire's own frustration seemed to mount. "Not just *any* man. One you might like."

Olivia frowned at her sister, her lips pursed.

Claire tried again to make her sister understand. "One that your spying grandfather saw you with once. So do you see him yet? Stop giving me that look and just *read.*"

Olivia gazed down at the open program. Immediately a small black-and-white picture stood out in the middle the page. Garrett Krause.

A lump formed in her throat and she swallowed. Seeing Garrett again, even if only in a picture—how to describe the emotions building in her heart? The pleasure. The pain. The excitement. The remorse. The need. The regret.

But wait—just what was he doing here? "He hates these things," Olivia accidentally said aloud.

"And so do you," Claire said with a wide, relieved smile that indicated she was thrilled her sister finally got what was happening. "Sounds like kismet to me."

Olivia stilled as the full impact of tonight washed over her. "I've been set up. My entire family set me up."

"Only to a point. *He* doesn't know *you're* here," Claire said. She raised her number as the bidding for Cliff Jones began.

"Thank God," Olivia said. "It's over between us. I can't just buy him and start right back up. That would be foolish."

Claire's arm shot up again and she glared at the woman outbidding her. "That darn Samantha Parker. I should have known."

Claire's arm kept going up and down as Olivia fidgeted in the seat beside her. Her family had set her up; well, at least Grandpa Joe and Claire had. It was doubtful her father was in on this, and Sara would certainly disapprove.

So maybe tonight could be a chance to redeem herself, an opportunity to set things right, clean up the ugliness. Or maybe she should simply sneak away before anyone was the wiser.

"Because it's not like he knows I'm here," Olivia said aloud to reassure herself.

"Sold to number five-fifty," the auctioneer announced. Triumphant, Claire lowered her number. On stage, Cliff was close enough to see who'd bought him, and Claire gave him a friendly wave. He grinned, and his eyes widened when his gaze landed on Olivia.

Olivia froze. *No. This didn't just happen.* She'd been spotted, and if she left now, she'd be acting like a spineless coward.

As Cliff exited the stage with his group, Claire sighed her satisfaction and sipped her wine. "Sorry, kid sister, but Grandpa Joe did a little research. That's Garrett's friend, isn't it?"

"Yes," Olivia said, understanding why her cousin Darci had always muttered, "If I didn't love Grandpa Joe, I'd…"

Her grandfather was a professional meddler, and if he had been sitting next to her at that moment, Olivia would have wrung his neck with her bare hands.

Claire's next words confirmed Olivia's fear. "Don't

kill the messenger, sweetie, and I didn't buy him just because of you—not even *I* would go that far. But I'd say Garrett's about to learn you're here."

Lovely, was Olivia's only thought. *Just lovely.*

Chapter Thirteen

"What do you mean Olivia's here?" Garrett stared at Cliff, sure he hadn't heard him correctly.

Unfortunately he had.

"She's sitting in the first row to your right when you walk out onstage," Cliff said. "Her sister Claire just bought me. I went for three thousand five hundred."

"Not bad, Cliff," someone called.

"The disc jockey got four," someone else teased.

"Yeah, well, his date came with an offer to pick all the songs on the radio station for an hour. Who could resist that?" Cliff said with a laugh.

"So Olivia's here?" Garrett repeated. He wasn't sure how to take the news. He'd tried to bury her memory these past few weeks—unsuccessfully.

"Of course she's here. If you had read your program, you'd see that as Jacobsen's representative, she opened the event."

"I guess that makes sense," Garrett said. During his research into her father and her family, he'd learned that another of her lies had been her job. She was a vice president in her family firm.

As for the event or its program, Garrett hadn't been interested in reading the profiles of the other guys in the room. He was doing the auction for Moira. The BackStoppers had been good to her, and tonight's proceeds went entirely to the worthy organization.

The men being auctioned off hadn't been in the grand ballroom at the start of the event. They'd been ensconced in a smaller ballroom until it was time for them to take the stage. After the bidding ended, they'd be free to meet their purchasers. But Garrett now found himself interested that Olivia was here. He hadn't seen her since the morning he learned of Pete's death, and he hadn't slept well since then. Despite washing all his sheets, he could still sense her presence.

"You said her sister bought you?" Garrett asked.

"Yep," Cliff said. "I'm not sure why. I have to say, I've heard great things about Claire Jacobsen, but I've never met her."

"How did Olivia seem?" Garrett asked before he could stop himself. He found himself curious. Would she have recovered already? He certainly hadn't. Funny, how after Pete's death she was the one who probably would have understood—and she was the last person he could call.

"She seemed fine," Cliff said. "I didn't really have a chance to scrutinize her. The lights are pretty blinding when you're onstage. You'll see when you get out there, and afterward if she buys you."

"She's probably not here to bid on me," Garrett said. "If I know Olivia, she probably had no idea I was doing this auction."

"Garrett, do you like her?" Cliff's voice was sharp and serious, and Garrett stilled.

"Who—Olivia?" he asked.

"Yes, Olivia," Cliff said, his "you dunce" obvious in his tone.

"I do," Garrett said slowly. He could admit that, had admitted it to himself several times since their break-up. "But I don't know why. I told her to get out of my life, so why do I keep thinking about her?"

Cliff's expression gentled. "Sometimes love's like that. Maybe you should just go for it. Even if she doesn't bid on you."

"I have your approval now?" Garrett's skepticism was obvious. And had Cliff mentioned *love*?

Cliff sighed. "You never needed my approval. I was worried about you being miserable. I didn't want her to hurt you, and I judged her based on her past. But I'm starting to believe that you're worse off without her. Maybe you *should* date her. Maybe she's your other half. She sure seems like it, the way you've been acting lately. Perhaps I was wrong in warning you away from her. You're capable of making your own decisions."

"I don't know if she's my other half," Garrett said. "I hardly know her."

"You saw what she did for Moira," Cliff said. "Blake Jacobsen does a lot of funerals, but I've never heard of him rearranging his international travel schedule for one. I think, Garrett, that all along you've connected with Olivia on the level where it really counts. You know her in your heart."

Garrett thought about that for a moment. He'd known her fundamental personality the moment he met her, when she'd been dressed like a schoolgirl. She'd blushed—she'd been trying to be something she wasn't.

What she was was the woman who'd cooked him dinner, who'd spent the day at the park with him, who'd dropped everything and babysat Matt just because Garrett had asked her to. Olivia's parents were ministers, and they'd raised her to be honest. She had wanted to tell him everything; he remembered those words clearly now. Her good intentions had always been there.

Garrett's sixth sense had grasped Olivia Jacobsen and all her hopes and fears. He had known her as if he'd grown up with her all his life. He'd connected with her immediately, as if fate said he was supposed to be with her. They'd been two people destined to meet. She was the one. Destiny could be scary that way, especially when human emotions got involved and started to muck everything up.

Maybe tonight could be about second chances. In a fundamental way, he'd bonded with Olivia. He'd been her first lover, as if that had also been ordained. In a caveman sense, that had made her his woman. He'd groveled once; perhaps tonight was the night to get down on his knees metaphorically and beg again.

"Blue group, you're up," the woman serving as room mom said. She wore a headset and had a small radio transmitter at her waist.

"That's you," Cliff told Garrett. "Go make the most of it."

"I'm ready," Garrett said and headed to the ballroom door. He paused for a moment and glanced at the bank of video monitors. Live feed showed that the ballroom was packed and the stage empty. It was his group's turn. Olivia was out there. Would she bid on him, though? And if she didn't, should he still approach her afterward? Nervousness consumed him and he tried to bury it. He was a cop, and a good one; cops were supposed to be cool under pressure.

He got into line: two people in front, two in back. They would hit the stage in the order found in the program.

"Okay, get out there," the woman told them, and sent them on their way.

Garrett took a breath and the line began to move.

"SEE ANYTHING you like now?" Claire said as Garrett walked onto the stage. "Because if you do, I could definitely understand why you might keep your promise and act on it."

Olivia's hands shook. Already the ballroom had erupted into cheers of delight. She didn't want to tear her gaze from Garrett, but she had to find out what he'd offered as his date. She skimmed the auction program. All the men were from that charity calendar. She quickly read his bio. He hadn't promised anything aside from dinner.

The way the women were reacting, no one seemed to care what any of these men had offered.

The auctioneer's arms stretched wide as he gestured to the crowd. "I can tell you ladies like what you see, so let's open your wallets wide for our Hometown Heroes. We'll start with Mark Williams. He's a fire-fighter…"

Olivia tuned out the auction. She could do this. No, she couldn't. Her nerves stretched taut. "I think I need the ladies' room," she told Claire.

"You do not," Claire snapped. "For once, Olivia Jacobsen, you are going to do what's best for you, not what's best for everyone else."

Claire's words raised Olivia's ire. "And how do you know that buying him is best for me? Neither you nor my grandfather knows what went on between us. It ended badly. It's over. Garrett is probably hoping that I *don't* bid on him. If I were him, I would."

"Grandpa Joe said you're in love with him and he's never wrong."

"He said what?" Olivia's mouth dropped open. "You two have even been talking in depth about my love life? Some things should be sacred!"

"No. Well, yes." Claire at least had the decency to be sheepish. "I told you this was a setup. Grandpa Joe recognized Garrett from the calendar the day he dropped you off around seven-thirty. Remember? Sara had a party that you bagged? I'm the only sibling who went. So Grandpa tracked me down, since I'd done the calendar. Olivia, our grandfather is the ultimate busybody and matchmaker whose heart is in the proper place. He only wants you to be happy. Do you think you really had to be here tonight, when I could have filled your role? I am a Jacobsen. I've opened restaurants. I could have done this gala, especially since I'm on the fund-raising committee."

"So you're saying that Grandpa Joe spent a fortune on me? He underwrote this thing to get me here?" The thought created a sense of sheer wonder and irate disbelief that her grandfather would go this far just to matchmake.

"It's for charity, and he has nothing else to do with his millions. I'd say he watched enough that day to see what he considered your perfect match."

The spirited bidding had ended at forty-five hundred dollars for the firefighter. "I don't like people manipulating me," Olivia said. "If he put me here to bid on Garrett, I'm not going to do it."

"Suit yourself," Claire said. "You're in charge of your destiny, you and only you. Grandpa Joe just thought you could use a push. Just because everyone else succumbed to his meddling doesn't mean that you have to."

"I'm moving to New York," Olivia said with a determined jut of her jaw. "I'm taking a position at O'Brien Publications." But even as she said the words, she could hear them for what they really were. A cop-out. She was running away instead of addressing her problems.

She'd been a passive bystander in her own life. Most women were. They dreamed, but they didn't scheme. They were the good girls, the ones who conformed. They weren't the gutsy girls ready to risk everything for the brass ring, but the nice girls who eventually wondered why life had passed them by. And if the bad girls missed their target? They picked themselves up, dusted themselves off and tried again. The good girls simply saved face and hid their tears. At that moment Olivia knew that the reason her life was so boring was that she'd let it become that way.

"Next up is Garrett Krause, Mr. August in Hometown Heroes." At the auctioneer's words the crowd applauded enthusiastically. "Shall we start at five hundred?"

Olivia glanced around the ballroom. She couldn't count the placards waving in the air. Garrett would not be embarrassed. He'd go for quite a lot of money. Already the bidding was at two thousand and rising up in two-hundred-dollar increments.

"If you're planning to bid you should do it soon," Claire prodded.

"It's my life," Olivia reminded her.

"Fine," Claire said. "Are you telling me that this isn't the man you really want? Isn't the man you love?"

"You…" Olivia couldn't say the words. She couldn't lie and say, You know he isn't. Because Garrett was.

And this man, the one she loved, stood on the stage about fifteen feet away. He was smiling at the crowd, but Olivia could tell his mood was faked.

Dear Lord, but Garrett must hate this. Even though he remained smiling, that pulling-teeth expression was back.

The first time she'd met him, he hadn't wanted to be placing a personal ad, either. She'd saved him then, and admittedly, he'd saved her right back. She could do this. It was time to atone for her past by jump-starting her future. An idea took root. She would do what was honorable and decent by her standards, not everyone else's.

Olivia leaped to her feet, the wooden stick solid in her hand. Garrett was at three thousand one hundred dollars. She held up her number and a chill ran down her spine. "Ten thousand."

The auctioneer sputtered for a moment, tripping over his excessively fast speech. "Did you say…ten thousand dollars?"

Olivia straightened her arm and shoving her number forward so he could read it better. "That's what I said. Ten thousand dollars."

In the smaller banquet room, Cliff had moved to the live-feed monitors. The sound was low, but he could hear what had just been said and see what had just happened.

"Holy—" Mason said as he stood on tiptoe to get a view over Cliff's shoulder.

"No cursing," Cliff said, although quite frankly, he'd like to say a few choice words himself. Who knew Olivia Jacobsen had such spunk?

"Okay, number five-fifty-one bids ten thousand. Do I hear ten thousand one hundred?" The auctioneer pointed. Someone had bid ten thousand one hundred.

But as Cliff watched, Olivia wasn't about to be denied. She held her number card high. "Twelve thousand," she said. She turned to glare at the woman who had bid the ten thousand one hundred on Garrett. "Just in case you don't know who I am, I'm Olivia Jacobsen and I'm bidding in one-thousand-dollar increments. Can you keep up?"

"I can keep up," the woman said.

Cliff found himself coughing.

"Really?" Olivia said. She reached down and dragged out her checkbook. She waved the leather case in the air. "Because I'd advise against wasting your money. Didn't you see me up there earlier? My family firm underwrote this event. So if you want this man as much as I do, I might let you have him, but it's going to cost you one hell of a lot of money, high-five low-six figures minimum. Think about that. Do you really wish to go up against me when there are other men left to buy? Because I'm ready."

Olivia turned to the auctioneer, shoved her number forward again and upped her bid. "Twenty thousand, enough for a small compact car nicely loaded. That won't even put a dent in my checkbook. I'm not lying, am I, Claire?"

"No," Claire said, looking like she was choking out the words.

In the anteroom where the men waited, Cliff

watched with amazement. He would never play poker with Olivia. He had no doubt in his mind that she was serious. Serious about buying Garrett, and serious about being very much in love with him. Darn, but he'd judged her wrong.

The auctioneer recovered and said, "Number five-fifty-one bids twenty thousand. Do I hear twenty-one thousand?"

No one in the ballroom breathed as the auctioneer began, "Going once, going twice, sold to number five-fifty-one for twenty thousand. Next up we have Adam Brown. He's a detective with…"

OLIVIA SAT DOWN with a *thump*. Her whole body shook like a leaf in a hard rain.

"Wow," Claire said. "I never would have guessed you could be so forceful. Good to see that side of you. Must be that Greek blood we've got in our veins finally coming out."

"Yeah," Olivia said. The bidding for the two remaining men had ended and Garrett had left the stage. The other men had sold for less than six thousand each. "I'm sure my actions will be all over the paper tomorrow."

"So?" Claire didn't seem overly concerned.

"I just made an absolute fool of myself."

Claire grinned. "And it felt good, didn't it?"

"Actually, yeah," Olivia said. She could almost hear her inner bad girl cheering. Life was to be embraced with both hands.

"For what it's worth, I think it's about time," Claire

said. She craned her neck. "Oh, the kicker is up in the next group. Maybe I should try your technique if the bidding gets sticky."

"I'm off to pay for my purchase, then to the rest room." Olivia said. "I'll be back."

"If you decide to leave, call my cell. I want to know that you're home safe."

"I'm not leaving," Olivia said.

Claire's smug expression said it all. "Of course you aren't," she said. "Olivia Jacobsen never lies."

"Well…" Olivia said as she grabbed her purse and stood. "You'd be amazed at how many I've told lately."

"Exactly," Claire said. "So don't do anything I wouldn't do."

"You'd—" Olivia started.

"Exactly," Claire interjected with a knowing nod. "Call me when you're safely home."

Olivia made her way out of the ballroom and over to the tables set up for payment. She handed over her placard. "I owe you twenty thousand," she said.

"Yes, you do," the woman said. She wore a flustered expression as she took Olivia's placard and checked the number against the registration. "We really thank you for your bid, Ms. Jacobsen. Tonight's proceeds go to such a great cause. Your donation will help us exceed our goals."

Olivia toyed with her purse strap. "I assume my personal check is fine?"

"Of course," the woman said. She twisted her gold necklace while Olivia wrote out the check and put her driver's license number in the corner. "Thank you," the woman said as Olivia passed the contribution over.

Olivia returned her purse to her shoulder and headed toward the ladies room. Conversation in the ladies room ceased as she entered. Olivia drew her shoulders up and tried not to laugh at the women's curious and admiring expressions. Controlling one's destiny was like dancing in the rain. Exhilarating.

"Ladies," she said.

Several minutes later, Olivia left the rest room. She had one last thing to do. She entered the side hall used by the event staff, went straight up to a door and stepped inside. Men milled around. Most of them were eager to enter the ballroom the minute the auction was complete. They'd been cooped up for about an hour or so now, and despite available food and beverage, they were ready to be let loose.

"You're not supposed to be in here," the woman monitoring the door said, but Olivia simply held up her receipt and silenced her.

"I'd like to see Garrett Krause."

The sea of men parted, and then he was in view. He stood there in a black tux, the most gorgeous thing she'd ever seen. The black set off his blond hair and those amazing blue eyes. The woman-in-control-of-her-destiny faltered a little, but she'd come this far and would make it the rest of the way.

"Can we talk?" she asked him.

"Sure." Garrett headed toward her. The room monitor stepped aside and said nothing as the two of them left.

"I'm sorry if I embarrassed you," Olivia said. "I know how much you hate these things, so I couldn't let anyone else buy you."

"It was okay. I might be the talk of the town, but you made me the highest bid of the night," Garrett said. His lips crooked into a small grin. "That earns a lot of respect from the testosterone set in there. Besides, I found it interesting to view that side of you."

"It comes from having a Greek mother. I guess I did inherit some of her passion. I found out I wasn't so passive after all."

"No one would doubt that after witnessing tonight's display," Garrett said. "Cliff told me you were here. I didn't think you were going to bid."

"I almost didn't," she admitted. "My family set me up. They knew you were going to be here. They told me to buy something I wanted. But…that's not why I bought you." Olivia clutched her purse tighter. "You're free."

Garrett halted abruptly, and Olivia walked past him. "What do you mean?" he asked her.

She stopped and turned around, the distance providing a smidgen of safety for what she had to do. "When you first walked into the *Monitor* office, you needed one date. You didn't want to be there any more than you wanted to be onstage tonight. You did this only because of Pete and Moira."

"True. But what does that have to do with anything?"

"You're not ready to be out in the dating game yet, Garrett. And the least I could do was put a stop to what we should have put a stop to the day we met. Your bio promised one date. I've had three. Go in peace, Garrett."

He took a step forward. "You paid twenty thousand dollars to ease your conscience?"

"No. I paid to ease yours. You are so worth every penny, and God forbid, I hope the BackStoppers never have to someday show up at your wife's house."

He'd moved back into her proximity, and his disbelief rolled off him in waves. "You don't want the date?"

Of course she did! But they weren't meant to be, and she accepted that. The hardest thing Olivia had ever done was shake her head. "Garrett, I'm most likely moving to New York City in November to take a job with O'Brien Publications. What I want and what I can have are two different things. However, tonight proved one thing. I could set this town on its ear and let myself loose. And I could let you loose at the same time. I owed you that."

She attempted to smile, her heart breaking as she said the words she didn't want to say but finally had the courage to say. Olivia Jacobsen had grown up, and the good girl and the bad girl had become one. "Give my hellos to Matt. Goodbye, Garrett."

With that she strode toward the hotel lobby.

Chapter Fourteen

"You are going after her, aren't you?"

Garrett pivoted. Cliff stood there in the glaring lights of the hallway. "Did you have to eavesdrop?"

"It's called being a witness," Cliff said with a grin that faded quickly. "And, yes, to protect your butt, I did have to."

Garrett practically growled. "My rear doesn't need protecting."

"Maybe not, but it sure as hell needs kicking. Go after her."

Garrett tossed up his hands, a gesture marking the futility he felt. "She's moving to New York. What type of relationship are we supposed to have?"

Cliff's expression remained disbelieving. "A hot one? One that's full of love and passion? Garrett, are you so blind and jaded that you can't tell she's deeply in love with you?"

"In love with…" Garrett parroted the words, allowing them to sink in a little.

"Duh," Cliff chastised. "She just wrote a check for twenty-thousand dollars. Enough for a small compact car, nicely loaded, I think I heard her say."

"But how does that prove—"

"Garrett, she loves you. You. Olivia Jacobsen, Miss 'I do nothing that might embarrass my parents', just made a scene in a ballroom over you. She'll make every gossip column in the *Post-Dispatch* and be the highlight of local radio. And she acted up just so you didn't have to go on a date with anyone else or with her? If you believe that, I've got a bridge to sell you."

"But I…" Garrett faltered as suppressed emotions began to surface.

"What? Don't love her?" Cliff said the words Garrett had been afraid to say. "No, maybe you don't love her yet, but you will. You've already fallen for her. Hard. It's just a matter of time before you admit to yourself that she might be worth risking everything for, that she just might be the woman for you."

Garrett had thought all those things earlier, but a man didn't go down without one final swing. "Boy, you sure have changed your tune where she's concerned."

Cliff shrugged in defeat. "Yeah, well, at least I realize when to eat crow. You're still trying to season your mistakes and pass them off. So, are you going after her or what?"

"I don't know where she's headed."

Cliff gazed heavenward, as if seeking help from the divine. "And you're a detective. Sometimes you can be so dense. She's Olivia Jacobsen. She just made a scene. It's not rocket science to guess she's going home. I'm betting you have a good idea where that is."

"I do," Garrett said.

"Well." Cliff gave a big grin. "Case closed."

GARRETT DROVE into Olivia's driveway, but the Saab was missing. He pounded his fist on the wheel in frustration. "So much for her being home! Good detective work, Cliff."

He gazed at the clock on the dashboard. It was almost eleven-fifteen. He sighed. He'd had the entire drive from downtown to think about what he was going to say, and now that she wasn't here, all his ideas had flown out the driver's side window. He reached for the door handle. His legs could use a quick stretch.

He climbed out of the car. In the distance he could hear the pool gurgling. He tilted his head up, taking in the stars. A sliver of moon winked against the blackness of the night sky and his feet crunched over the gravel as he strode toward the gate. He paused at the wrought iron, looking at the blackened water beyond.

Here was a world so unfamiliar to him. He'd grown up in a house maybe fifteen hundred square feet in size. His flat was smaller. Olivia's pool house had over two thousand square feet. But where they lived or how they lived was the least of his problems. Right now he had to win her over, to prove that things could work out between them. That was what he wanted, he knew that now, and he wasn't about to be denied again.

The sound of an engine alerted him, and he walked back to his car. He could see Olivia's shocked expression in the reflection of her headlights as the beams bounced off his trunk. She stopped, killed the engine and opened the door.

"Hi," he said as she exited the Saab.

"Hi," she said, her hesitation obvious. "What are you doing here?"

As she stepped closer, Garrett realized how dead-on he'd been. This was his woman, the one he wanted. "I believe we have a date."

"I already explained," she said.

Garrett pointed to the sky. "You told me, but I don't believe you explained your decision to Him."

"Meaning?"

"Fate," Garrett said. "Or some force that neither of us can deny. A pull. An attraction. A predestination if you want to go that far."

"I don't know that I care to," Olivia said. She shifted her weight.

Garrett stood his ground. He'd suspected that convincing her wasn't going to be easy. They'd been through so much in so little time, and they had not been very honest with their feelings, either to each other or themselves. They'd been unintentionally cruel.

"Then to what would you credit this attraction?"

"I have no idea." She slapped at a bug. "At least come inside. The critters are out."

"Ah, she invites me in."

She turned. "Would you rather be eaten alive?"

"Not really," he said, his momentary humor fading. This was certainly unfamiliar territory. He followed her to the side door. "I like your outfit by the way."

"Thanks."

"It's rare that one finds a woman who doesn't rationalize a compliment. Do you know that's one thing I like about you? How rare you are and how different from others? I'm glad you wore yellow. It suits you."

"I was a tad underdressed," Olivia admitted. "Everyone was in black."

"In my opinion you're overdressed," Garrett said as they stepped into the kitchen. "And black's overrated."

"What's gotten into you?" Olivia said. She turned around.

"Actually, you have," Garrett replied. "You're right. If any other woman had bought me, I would have hated it. If any other woman had stood up there and done what you did, I would have been mortified. But you became my buyer, and how you went about defending what was yours fascinated me. Everything about you fascinates me. I can't imagine ever being bored. And you're the only woman who has ever managed to take each one of my deal breakers and flip them on their ear."

"Deal breakers?" She switched on two more light switches, flooding the entire living area with light.

He nodded. "Yes. The one thing a person can do that ends the relationship. It can be as simple as being too possessive, calling too much, taking things too fast…or an annoying habit that suddenly gets on your nerves and drives you nuts."

"Oh, I'd just never heard them called deal breakers." But she understood what they were. Flaws. Her own list had been miles long, until Garrett.

"Olivia, there are no deal breakers with you. You had secrets, and I didn't mind. I wanted to be with you. I still do."

"That Saturday…"

"That Saturday we both mucked things up, me probably more than you. Cliff had warned me that you were like Brenda. But you aren't. You're generous."

"I'm selfish," Olivia contradicted him.

Garrett shook his head. They were still standing in the kitchen. "There's a fine line between being generous and being selfish. It's like that line between love and hate. Generous people often reap the benefits of their generosity. You helped Moira by talking to your father."

"That was the first unselfish thing I'd done," Olivia said. She leaned against the counter for support.

"And tonight you bought me and let me go," Garrett said.

"Second thing."

"Which is two more than none," Garrett said, "and that sets you apart from my ex-wife. You aren't like her, Olivia."

"No?"

"No," Garrett said, both tenderness and passion warming his body. "Not at all. If you were, I never would have said yes to your proposition, one date or not."

"Oh."

"You've become monosyllabic."

"I don't know what to say. I've…"

But Garrett did. He was ready to win this woman who'd captured his heart. "We've both wasted a lot of time being full of pride and protecting our own egos. I care about you, Olivia. A lot. It's too soon for me to tell you that I love you. If I said the words now, they would ring false or sound desperate. But I refuse to waste any more time. I want you in my life, more than anything. I think we can make a go of this. You. Me. Together."

"I'm moving—"

"Then our relationship will be a lot harder than if you lived here," Garrett said. "But we'll manage somehow."

Olivia's blue eyes remained unblinking as she comprehended his words. "You care about me that much?"

"More," Garrett said, and he did. "I've had four weeks without you, and I didn't like any of them. Cliff even told me that you are good for me after all. He's now solidly in your court."

"My sister bought him," Olivia said.

"And that should be an interesting date," Garrett said. "Should I worry about Cliff?"

"Probably," Olivia said with a little laugh that diffused the growing tension.

"It's what he deserves," Garrett said. "The nosy meddler."

"Speaking of meddling, you haven't met my grandfather yet. He's behind me being there tonight."

"Then I have to thank him," Garrett said.

"He spent a small fortune making things happen."

"Then I owe him a great deal." Garrett approached Olivia and drew her into his arms. Holding her again felt so good. "Don't leave me. As of tonight, we can start over. A new beginning."

Olivia gazed up at him, hope evident. "I can't live with you," she said. Her bottom lip quivered. "In reality, I'm not that kind of girl."

Garrett lowered his lips to Olivia's and pressed one kiss against her mouth. "Darling, I value honesty. I also have too much respect for your father and wouldn't like to end up in your mother's column. I have a strong suspicion that making you an honest woman is very much around the corner. I can think of nothing in my future that I'd like better."

"Promises, promises," Olivia said.

"Absolutely." He placed her hand on his heart. "I'm not going to say those words for reasons previously outlined, but tell me you can sense how I feel."

"I can," she said. His heart beat under her fingers, thumping evidence of how much he cared. Joy at being loved by the right man completed her.

"Now, give me some of your goodness and kiss me. Our relationship won't be easy, with my erratic shifts and your move, but we'll adapt. I want nothing more than to be with you."

"Did you ever see *Tombstone?*" Olivia asked, wishing to get back to the kissing he'd mentioned first.

"Yeah. With Kurt Russell as Wyatt Earp."

She warmed to her point. "So far so good. And what did his girlfriend Josie tell him at the end, when he finally came to win her back?"

Garrett laughed. "Not to worry—her family was rich."

"You'll need some time to get used to my money, but we'll work through any conflicts," she said, in her mind already crossing the move to New York off her list.

"I don't want to be a 'what's mine is yours' type of guy," Garrett said. "I'm not coming into this with much."

"And we'll deal with this issue together. I can't change my family or my past, but I promise to make it insignificant. Or at least keep you very diverted."

"If that means you'll finally kiss me now, that could be step one," Garrett said.

Technically, he was the one who'd digressed from the topic first. But who cared? Finally, he could kiss her. And so Olivia obliged him, and they reveled in the kiss that was the beginning of a whole new life.

GRANDPA JOE SURVEYED his Thanksgiving table. Eighteen people sat comfortably in his dining room. Nick and Maxie had arrived in town, and Maxie's parents were at the table. Nick and Maxie had made their announcement, and once everyone had gotten over their initial surprise, the champagne had flowed and congratulations had abounded. Sara couldn't have been more thrilled, and she'd already turned her eye to her two daughters. Claire had been dating Cliff Jones since the bachelor auction, and they were all was holding their collective breath to see if that worked out. Joe had an inkling it would; the two were both so strong-willed that they balanced each other and that kept the excitement and harmony.

Joe gazed the length of the table and he winked at his wife. Henrietta smiled back, a secret smile of two people who'd been one for over fifty years. He'd created a legacy, and he was content. At the table sat his daughter, Lilly, and his son Blake, and their respective spouses, Andrew and Sara. The other grandchildren were there, as well: Shane and his wife, Lindy; Bethany and her crew; and Harry and his wife, Megan. In the other room, at the traditional kids table, sat all his great-grandchildren, even the babies. The only grandchild missing was Darci, and she was in New York at her husband's family's house. Yes, Joe was indeed blessed. He had the greatest riches in the world—his family.

"So when do you think you'll get the other two wed?" Andrew, his son-in-law and president of Jacobsen Enterprises, leaned over and asked, his voice low so that no one else could overhear. The men had become great friends over the years.

Joe grinned. "I told you about the bachelor auction."

"We all know that you pull everyone's strings. You're the ultimate matchmaker. When will Blake have to officiate for the last two?"

Joe glanced down the table. Olivia and Garrett had

their heads bent close together. "I'd say within the next year. Why? Do you want to bet?"

Andrew shook his head. "I've learned you always take my money."

Joe sighed. "It's a dirty job, but someone has to do it."

To his credit, Andrew just laughed.

"THAT WAS NICE," Olivia said. They were in Garrett's Malibu, heading back to his flat so they could put Matt to bed after the Thanksgiving dinner at her grandparents' estate. It was way past Matt's bedtime and he'd already fallen asleep in his booster seat.

"You survived your brother's announcement," Garrett said.

"Grandpa Joe told me earlier, and besides, I'm thrilled for Nick. I never have thought Maxie would be perfect for him, but seeing them together proves it. When you find your match, you just know."

"I did," Garrett said.

"Did not," Olivia said.

He laughed. "So it took me a while. You weren't so quick yourself."

"Touché."

When they arrived, Garrett parked his car and carried Matt upstairs to bed. Within moments, he and Olivia were alone in the living room. He reached for her hand.

"Have I told you how much I love you?"

"Not since right before dinner," Olivia said.

"Then I'm behind on today's quota."

"I love you," they said at the same time. They started laughing.

"Stop trying to beat me," Garrett said.

"Oh, I can beat you," Olivia said with a laugh. She playfully tried to punch his shoulder, but he caught her hand and gently pinned it to her chest.

"You forget I'm a cop. We're trained in self-defense." He leaned his head down to kiss her. "Time to pay the fine."

Olivia giggled and kissed him. "Seriously," she said. "I love you."

She did. They'd had their difficulties, but they'd committed to working through them. That meant addressing the money issue—what to pool and what to keep separate. It meant brainstorming where to live—they'd decided on residences on neutral territory in January, and had already found a house in Ballwin. It meant learning to deal with Brenda and being a stepmother to Matt. It also meant discussing how many children of their own they would have. They'd simply settled on "a lot," leaving it to fate for a beginning and, eventually, an end.

Contentment and desire combined as his lips lowered to her neck. It had taken Garrett only two weeks after the auction to find the perfect moment to tell her how much he loved her. She'd let him say the words first; after all, he'd known all along how she felt. It was on her face every time she looked at him.

"So, Christmas," Garrett said at the end of the kiss. "Do you think that's a good time to tell our families?"

Olivia moved her neck out of his reach. "That what—we ran away last weekend and got married in Vegas?"

He grinned sheepishly. "Well, yeah. I know you didn't want to steal your brother's thunder by saying anything tonight, but your stepmother was giving me the evil eye at dinner. She still isn't used to us living at each other's places."

Olivia laughed. "Wait until you see what she'll do once she realizes that she can't plan my wedding. Nevertheless, she's very happy for us. She told me so tonight."

"Maybe we should have your dad do a ceremony anyway," Garrett said. "Just a small one. You'd like that, wouldn't you? One that's more spiritual then legal?"

She would. Their decision to run away and get married had been spur-of-the-moment. And it had eased their consciences. Besides, by eloping, they'd created their own personal space to become a permanent couple before the world shared in their joy. The simple silver band she wore on her left hand might pass as a dinner ring, but they both knew better.

"Okay, at Christmas," Olivia agreed. "We'll tell only my dad so he can prepare a ceremony. He's good at keeping secrets. So is my grandfather for the most part. They'd love to pull a secret wedding off without their wives knowing. Grandpa Joe will of course clamor to host our event at his house."

"Christmas, then, and no later. My family will be

in town this year. All I have to do is tell them to show up and the entire Krause clan will be there." Garrett lowered his mouth to hers again. "Now that the hubbub with your brother is over, and his wedding isn't for a while, I want the whole world to know."

"That sounds good and I agree," she said between kisses.

Garrett reached for her hand, and she placed it trustingly in his. "And you once thought we wouldn't be able to blend our worlds," he said.

"We didn't. We created a new one."

He smiled at her then, his blue eyes reflecting all the love he held in his heart. He lifted her hand to his lips. "I love you," he said. "My Mrs. Right."

"Always and forever," Olivia said, and with that, she let him sweep her away to the place where dreams do come true.

* * * * *

Don't miss THE MARRIAGE CAMPAIGN,
the first book in Michele Dunaway's
AMERICAN BEAUTIES miniseries.
Coming in August 2006 from
Harlequin American Romance.

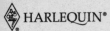
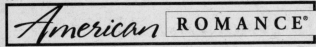

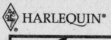

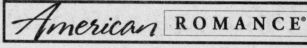

A THREE-BOOK SERIES BY

Kaitlyn Rice

Heartland Sisters

To the folks in Augusta, Kansas, the three sisters
were the Blume girls—a little pitiable, a bit mysterious
and different enough to be feared.

The three sisters may have received an odd upbringing,
but there's nothing odd about the affection, esteem
and support they have for one another, no matter
what the crises that come their way.

THE THIRD DAUGHTER'S WISH

When Josie Blume starts to search for the father she's
never known, she's trying to lay some family ghosts to rest.
Other surprises are in store on her journey back into time—
and one of them is rediscovering Gabe Thomas, a man who
shares not only her past and present but her future, too.

Available June 2006

Also look for:

THE LATE BLOOMER'S BABY
Available October 2005

THE RUNAWAY BRIDESMAID
Available February 2006

Available wherever Harlequin books are sold.

www.eHarlequin.com

Home improvement has never seen results like this!

When she receives a large inheritance, Stacy Sommers decides she is finally going to update her kitchen. Her busy husband has never wanted to invest in a renovation, but now has no choice. When the walls come down, things start to change in ways that neither of them ever expected.

Finding Home

by Marie Ferrarella

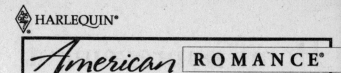

HARLEQUIN®

American ROMANCE®

**IS DELIGHTED TO BRING YOU FOUR BOOKS
IN A MINIERIES BY POPULAR AUTHOR**

Jacqueline Diamond

Downhome Doctors
First-rate doctors
in a town of second chances

DAD BY DEFAULT
On sale June 2006

In Dr. Connor Hardison's view, unwed mothers—and
that includes his lovely nurse—aren't responsible
enough to raise children. Until the death of a former
girlfriend unexpectedly makes him a single father
with a four-year-old son. And makes him question his
prejudices, too…

Also look for:

THE POLICE CHIEF'S LADY
On sale December 2005

NINE-MONTH SURPRISE
On sale February 2006

A FAMILY AT LAST
On sale April 2006

Available wherever Harlequin books are sold.

They were twin sisters with nothing in common…

Until they teamed up on a cross-country adventure to find their younger sibling. And ended up figuring out that, despite buried secrets and wrong turns, all roads lead back to family.

Sisters

by Nancy Robards Thompson

Available June 2006
TheNextNovel.com

This riveting new saga begins with

In the Dark

by national bestselling author

JUDITH ARNOLD

The party at Hotel Marchand is in full swing when the lights suddenly go out. What does head of security Mac Jensen do first? He's torn between two jobs—protecting the guests at the hotel and keeping the woman he loves safe.

A woman to protect. A hotel to secure. And no idea who's determined to harm them.

On Sale June 2006

**Four sisters.
A family legacy.
And someone is out to destroy it.**

**A captivating new limited
continuity, launching June 2006**

The most beautiful hotel in New Orleans,
and someone is out to destroy it. But mystery,
danger and some surprising family revelations
and discoveries won't stop the Marchand sisters
from protecting their birthright…
and finding love along the way.